"I've already ma[de] other arrangements."

Josie's stunned look was replaced by one of fury. How dared he? Without so much as a "do you mind?" Kade had adjusted affairs to suit his purpose, making her feel like a puppet.

"Do you always expect people to jump at your bidding?" she demanded furiously.

The mocking light was still in his eyes as he replied softly, "Only when necessary, Miss West, and I think," he added in that maddening drawl, "you'll eventually see that my arrangement is suitable all around."

Josie's chin jutted out in defiance. Mr. High and Mighty Boston might think everything was settled, but it wasn't— not by a long shot!

OTHER
Harlequin Romances
by JANE CORRIE

Many of these titles are available at your local bookseller
or through the Harlequin Reader Service.

For a free catalogue listing all available Harlequin Romances,
send your name and address to:

HARLEQUIN READER SERVICE,
M.P.O. Box 707, Niagara Falls, N.Y. 14302
Canadian address: Stratford, Ontario, Canada N5A 6W2

or use order coupon at back of book.

The Texan Rancher

by

JANE CORRIE

Harlequin Books

TORONTO • LONDON • NEW YORK • AMSTERDAM
SYDNEY • HAMBURG • PARIS

Original hardcover edition published in 1978
by Mills & Boon Limited

ISBN 0-373-02194-1

Harlequin edition published September 1978

Printed in Canada

CHAPTER ONE

JOSIE WEST watched as the cheerful bus driver took her cases out of the hold at the back of the bus, and placing them on the dusty ground on the outskirts of the small township, airily waved aside the tip she had wanted to give him and gave her a grin. 'There's sure to be some form of transport to take you the rest of the way.' he assured her cheerfully, and with a final wave seated himself back in the driver's seat. started up, and in a cloud of dust was on his way back towards the main highway.

Josie pocketed the tip, wishing the man had taken it, for he had earned it, coming as he had way off his regular route to put her down nearer to her destination. As for the transport he had so cheerfully assured her would be forthcoming, Josie had her doubts, and her eyes narrowed against the glare of the midday sun as she looked ahead of her to what she knew was the main street of the sleepy township tucked away in the furthermost part of east Texas. Not only the main street, but the only street, and Josie's brow furrowed as she tried to recall earlier memories of the town she had been born in, twenty-two years ago, the last twelve having been spent in England, being brought up by an aunt of hers whom her grandfather had sent her to stay with while receiving an education.

Memories flooded back to her, not of the township she was now looking towards, but of the

thriving market garden her grandfather had run.
Of the rows of greenhouses, and acres of planted
land—of fruit trees, and flowering shrubs, of the
games she used to play with Dan Muntrose's children, for he was her grandfather's manager of the
large concern. She sighed; it was odd really how
memories returned once she was back on familiar
ground. The candy store at the end of the street
was where she would rush at the end of the week to
spend the money her grandfather had allotted her,
depending on the week's behaviour, and how she
would always try to beat Nat, Dan's oldest son, to
the counter to be served first, although Nat was
seven years older than her, and nearly always won
the race hands down.

She wondered if Dan was still with her grandfather. Nat would presumably be married now, she
mused, for twelve years was a long time. Her lips
pressed together. Too long, she thought sadly, and
so much to make up for... She shook her head
impatiently, and stared down at her heavy cases.
Her grandfather's home lay just beyond the township; too far for her to walk carrying her cases, and
somehow she would have to get transport. She
could, of course, ring through and ask her grandfather to send a car to collect her, but she did not
want to do this—she wanted to walk in unan-
nounced, and tell him she was back to stay, and she
would have been back before if only she had
known what she knew now, and hope he would
understand and not be bitter at what must have
appeared to be hurtful neglect of his feelings in
the past.

The sound of horse's hoofs brought her out of

her musings, and she glanced round at the rider moving towards her, obviously going into the town. Considering that she had spent most of her life in a small Kentish village, the sight of a man on horseback, wearing a wide stetson and leather-fringed jacket, gave her no surprise, for this was cattle country, and when she was a child it had been a familiar sight, and awakened other memories of going to see rodeos with her grandfather; not that this man represented this kind of show; there were no dude ranches there. It was the real thing, and several flourishing ranches lay beyond the town. Cattle breeding was big business here.

The man reined in beside her, giving her a quick appraisal from under the stetson worn low over the forehead that almost obscured his features, but Josie caught a glimpse of weatherbeaten skin, and could almost feel his eyes taking in her slight form dressed in a cool green linen trouser suit that highlighted her corn-coloured hair, now pulled back in a pony tail to keep it tidy and away from her heart-shaped face.

'Lost?' he queried in a soft southern drawl, and Josie's wide blue eyes showed her amusement at the question as she answered smilingly, 'Not really, I was just wondering how to get some form of transport.'

The man pushed back his hat, and Josie saw that he was quite a lot younger than she had thought at first, in his early twenties, she guessed. His hair was longish and curled at the neck, and as his light blue eyes continued his scrutiny of her, he replied lightly, 'Guess it depends where you're heading.'

There was such a look of admiration in his eyes

that Josie felt embarrassed. She had seen that look before on a man's face, and though it ought to have pleased her feminine vanity, her shy nature abhorred such attention. His eyes told her he was quite willing to be of any assistance to her, she had only to name her objective.

'I'm heading for the Carella estate,' she told him. 'Joseph West is my grandfather. I expect you know him,' she added confidently. It was such a small place, the man was bound to know her grandfather.

The change in the man's manner was almost startling; he pushed his hat back on his head with a jerk, and his voice was no longer soft but hard and uncompromising as he jabbed a thumb towards the main street. 'Sure I know him,' he drawled. 'Just follow the white line, lady; eventually you'll come to it.'

With that terse direction, he spurred his horse into action and was soon galloping off, leaving an amazed Josie staring after him.

After a moment or so, she gave a wry grin. She had been given the brush-off in no uncertain manner, and it was a new experience for her. To give her credit, it did not shatter her, and her small chin was held high as she gazed after the man who had so abruptly dismissed her. He was probably the owner of a cattle ranch, she thought, and cattle men hadn't much time for market gardeners. He had probably tried to get her grandfather to part with some land and had come unstuck. She grinned again, imagining the short shrift such a request would be given by her grandfather, who was never one to mince his words.

Picking up her cases, she made her way towards the town, and went into the first store she came to. Apart from the horseman, she had not met one single soul. It was as if the place was deserted.

The chimes of the bell attached to the door were dwindling to a halt by the time someone appeared the other side of the counter of the grocery store, and Josie began to wonder if the town had been hit by some holocaust that had wiped out the population. Then she recalled that the noon hour was not an ideal time to make an appearance on an extremely hot day, and that the Spanish custom of taking a siesta still lingered in this part of the world.

As she watched the stout man in a white overall approach, she tried to recall whether she knew him or not, although she couldn't remember visiting this store when she was young, for all food would have been delivered to Carella. Even so, she searched for some recognition of the man now waiting to serve her, and came up with a complete blank. 'I'm sorry to trouble you,' she said, 'but is there any chance of hiring a taxi, or some form of transport to take me out to the Carella estate?'

Her blue eyes took in the man's reaction to this request, and it wasn't unlike the man on horseback's reaction, except for the curiosity that was only too apparent on his face, as he scratched his chin thoughtfully and remarked ponderously, 'Well, now, miss, that ain't exactly on the main route. Guess I do know of someone who might stretch a point and give you a lift out there, seeing he's short of the ready just now.' He gave Josie a searching look. 'Sure that's the place you want?' he queried hopefully.

Josie nodded abruptly, guessing the reason for the question. 'Mr West is my grandfather,' she replied, deciding to put the man out of his misery. 'I'd walk it, but I've my cases, you see.' She looked down at her cases, then back at the man. 'So if you would give me this man's address, or where I can contact him, I would be obliged to you.'

The grocer appeared to be having some difficulty in digesting Josie's disclosure, but pulled himself together in time to answer her. 'No problem there,' he drawled laconically, 'Marny will be where he always is at this time—at the pool room.'

At Josie's swift nod and stoop to collect her cases ready to go in search of the said Marny, he said hastily, 'Hang on—I'll see if I can raise him for you,' and turned to the telephone on the wall behind him.

Replacing her cases on the ground, Josie murmured her thanks and waited while the man dialled the number he wanted, and when connected, asked for the man in question. A few seconds later she heard him say, 'Got a lady here, Marny. Wants a lift out to Joe West's place.' After another short pause, he replaced the receiver and turned back to Josie. 'He's on his way,' he told her.

Thanking him once again, Josie walked to the door to await the transport, conscious all the time of the grocer's keen interest in her. One thing was certain, the man had not known of her existence, and that meant that he had taken the business after she had been sent to England. A slight frown creased her forehead; in a town this size, everybody knew everybody's business, and Josie's grandfather had been a prominent citizen in the town, so it was slightly odd that this man had not heard of her. His surprise and ensuing curiosity had been quite genuine, and it hurt Josie more than she cared to think.

Her eyes narrowed against the glare of the sun as she watched for the car. Twelve years was a long time—even longer, if no attempt had been made to communicate. Visits, of course, had been out of the question; Kent was a long way away from Texas. She gulped, and if the truth were known, she wouldn't be here now if certain facts hadn't come to light after her aunt's death a month ago.

There had not been much affection between Josie and her aunt, and it had often puzzled Josie as to why she had agreed to take her in the first place, for it was plain she was not what might be termed as 'motherly' in any sense of the word. Children were meant to be seen and not heard, and this sentiment was certainly enforced on young Josie, who grew up under the illusion that she ought to be grateful for the home she had been given, not to mention food and clothing.

Taking a handkerchief out of her jacket pocket, Josie wiped the perspiration off her forehead and hoped her grandfather had some form of air-conditioning. She wished she could remember more about the house she had stayed in before being sent to England. What she could remember with bitter clarity were her feelings at that tender age, at being sent away from the one person she had loved, her desolated feelings at the betrayal, for that was how she had viewed it at the time. Of her parents she had little recollection, but she must have loved them, and that love had been transferred with ferocious intensity to her 'Gramps', as she had called him, on their death in a railroad disaster. And there had been worse to come, as her bewildered tear-swollen eyes had alighted on the grim countenance of the woman waiting to collect her at the airport on her arrival in England.

Time had passed, and there had been no communication between her and her grandfather, and an unhappy child had had to accept the brusque, heartbreaking comment from her aunt, that her grandfather was much too busy to bother with her—he'd sent her away, hadn't he? because he couldn't be bothered with her, and she ought to be thanking her for taking her in, instead of whining for someone who didn't care any more.

The years had dulled the sorrow, and her memories had dimmed to vague shadows. Her aunt's death, however, had brought a very different picture of the past. For one thing, it had been her grandfather who had supported her all those years with regular payments to her aunt, thus revealing to Josie the real truth behind her so-called 'kindness' in taking her in, and for another, the payments had been of a more than generous nature. A conscience-stricken Josie had wondered how her aunt could have been so cruel as to keep her in ignorance of this fact all those years.

Josie had also found letters from her grandfather, sent to her aunt, in which he constantly asked for news of her. News which apparently was never given, as were the replies to the missives he had sent to Josie, for the simple reason that Josie had never received them, and her eyes had filled with tears as she sensed the bitterness behind his words when referring to her in later years.

She had taken particular note of the fact that the payments had stopped on her twenty-first birthday with a lump sum to be given, directed the letter in her grandfather's spidery writing, to Josie on her coming of age. Money that Josie had never received, nor ever would, for her aunt had willed her money to an obscure religious group with even obscurer objectives.

Had her aunt possessed a more tidy nature, or indeed had known that a stroll down to the local shops one morning would result in her death at the hands of a drunken driver losing control of his vehicle, she would no doubt have destroyed all trace of past payments. As it was, her habit of pushing all communications into the sideboard drawer and proceeding to forget them gave Josie an insight into the past, and a determination to make up for all those lost years, knowing that her grandfather must think she was very ungrateful for all his help, even though he didn't know that Josie had never benefited from it.

If it hadn't been for a premium bond win of five hundred pounds, she wouldn't have been able to make the trip out to Texas, for although she was now qualified as a teacher, she had only just qualified, and had been trying to obtain a post when her aunt had met her death. Subsequent revelations had made her more than ever anxious to obtain work of some nature, if only to enable her to save for the trip out there. She had had no intention of asking her grandfather to foot the bill; he had paid enough as it was.

A cloud of dust in the distance proclaimed the arrival of the transport Josie was waiting for, and collecting her cases, and smiling at the grocer who still stood watching her, she moved out of the doorway towards the car now drawing up beside her.

Marny proved very uncommunicative, and Josie gathered his mind was still on the game that he had had to abandon, and apart from making sure that he had got the destination right, he said little else until they had arrived, when he asked for two dollars for the trip.

Josie had been gazing a little bewilderedly at the sprawling but definitely dilapidated house they had drawn up beside, and her eyes searched for familiar scenes remembered from her childhood. Where were the lawns that once fronted the house? and where were the greenhouses that had once stood directly behind the house? For there was nothing there now but a wilderness of what had once been well-cared-for plants.

There was a hint of impatience in the man's voice as he repeated his request for the fare, and Josie shook herself out of her musings and fumbled in her purse for the money. It seemed a lot to pay for such a short journey, but nevertheless she paid it willingly, if only to get rid of the morose man by her side.

Without a 'thank you', or 'good afternoon' the man was on his way back to town by the time Josie had walked to the front door of the house.

On pushing the bell, and hearing no answering

echo within the house, Josie knocked on the door. Her mouth was dry, and all kinds of emotions were washing over her at that moment. Her grandfather must be ill, must have been for a long time to have let things get in this state—might even be dead! She swallowed. No, he couldn't be—the man in the store would have said so, wouldn't he? He wouldn't have let her come here without knowing that, would he? The thought somewhat calmed her, and on receiving no answer to her knocking, she left her cases on the front porch and walked round to the back of the house.

Passing along the side of the house, she heard voices coming from the back, and felt a surge of relief flow through her. The back of the house used to have a balcony that looked over the acres of land her grandfather owned, she recalled, and he was probably resting there.

The voices were louder as she approached the bend that led to the balcony, and Josie could hear what was being said, for one of the men talking had a vibrant voice, and a furious one. Her steps faltered to a stop, and she wasn't sure whether to wait or go on.

'I'm giving you one more chance,' bit out that cold voice. 'And it's more than you're entitled to. I'm sick and tired of cattle straying over that damned line. Before you know it, you won't have a roof over your head; it would take far less than a few steers to rock this place off its hinges. Okay, if that's the way you want to live, that's up to you. But don't come whining to me when you find yourself surrounded by several hundred herd. You've only yourself to blame. Why don't you do yourself a favour and sell up? Name your price; you won't find me quibbling over it. I'll give you a fair deal for the house as well, just as I did for the rest of the land. What do you say?'

Josie could not hear what her grandfather's reply had been, for it must have been her grandfather, but whatever it was, it didn't please his visitor. 'Then you'll just have to take the consequences,' he bit out furiously. 'But I'm warning you, if any of my herd gets poisoned on those blasted weeds you're too damned mean to pay someone to clear for you, then you'll be putting your hand into that long stocking of yours sooner than you think!'

The next minute the man had rounded the corner and almost cannoned into Josie, and she caught a glimpse of blazing grey eyes under a wide stetson before the man suddenly saw her and stopped dead in his tracks. 'Who the devil are you?' he rasped out, and before Josie had sufficiently recovered, went on bitingly, 'If you're selling anything, you've come to the wrong address. That old skinflint won't even give you the time of day!'

With eyes bright with indignation, Josie drew herself up to her full five feet two and met the blazing grey ones. 'I happen to be his granddaughter,' she said furiously. 'And I'll thank you to remember your manners in future! I heard what you said back there, and you ought to be ashamed of yourself, bullying an old man like that!' and with head held high, she brushed past the staring man as if he were of no consequence.

CHAPTER TWO

WHEN Josie got to the back porch, there was no sign of her grandfather. The balcony was still there, she noticed, but like the rest of the house, badly needing urgent repairs, with paintwork peeling off the rotting wood.

Slipping through the french windows that led to the balcony, she blinked a little as she entered the shaded room, then she saw him, sitting in what she remembered had been his favourite chair all those years ago.

'Gramps?' she said in a soft voice that threatened to choke into a sob, and as he turned towards her she saw that his sight was slightly impaired, for he had some difficulty in focusing on her.

The threatened sob escaped as she covered the distance between them, and flinging herself down beside him, she caught hold of his hand, murmuring brokenly, 'I didn't know, Gramps—I didn't know ...' and burst into tears.

It took a second or two for the old man to realise that it was indeed Josie, and his hand tightened on hers. 'It's okay, girl, it's okay,' he muttered as he passed a shaky hand over her hair. 'Guess you remembered me after all, huh?'

A little while later, when Josie was composed enough to speak coherently, she tried to tell him why she hadn't written, telling him of the kind of life she had led, praying he would understand how it had been. 'Aunt Babs never mentioned you, you see,' she said, swallowing the lump in her throat that seemed to get larger each time she looked at her grandfather, remembering how he had looked all those years ago; upright and proud, and with eyes as keen as a hawk's—now misty with age. 'I kept asking about you at first. I was so miserable at being sent away, and I never heard from you ...' she gulped. 'But you did write, didn't you? I found the letters afterwards. And all the time I thought you'd forgotten me ...' her voice petered out slowly.

His gnarled hand squeezed hers. 'So that's what happened,' he said half to himself, then sighed. 'They say one shouldn't speak ill of the dead, but by heaven, I wish she was here now!' he ground out. 'I wrote, child; each time I sent ...' he hesitated, and Josie guessed what he had been about to say—'the money'; however he changed it to 'wrote', and stared down at Josie's tear-stained face. 'I thought you'd forgotten me,' he said dryly, adding fiercely, 'Might have known that woman wouldn't keep her side of the bargain.'

Josie's eyes met his sad ones. 'Why did she do it, Gramps?' she asked quietly.

He shrugged his gaunt shoulders. 'Never forgave your mother, I guess; even though they were sisters. She loved your dad, too, see? Went sour with jealousy, and took off for England afore they were wed. Couldn't bear to see it happen.' He sighed. 'I thought that maybe after all those years she'd come round to it—but I guess she didn't.'

Josie held his hand to her wet cheek. 'If I hadn't had to go through her papers after she'd died, I wouldn't have known the truth,' she said, giving him a tremulous smile, and added fervently, 'Oh, I'm so glad I did! She'd kept your letters, you see, and I knew then that you hadn't forgotten me.' She gave him an accusing look. 'You stopped writing, and I was so afraid . . .' She gulped; there was no need to go on, he knew what she meant.

Giving her a lopsided grin, he said, 'Oh, there's life in the old dog yet,' then sobered. 'Saw no point in asking after you,' he stated gruffly. 'Couldn't get any replies, and as soon as . . .' He stopped again, and this time Josie finished the sentence for him.

'As I was twenty-one,' she said softly, firmly meeting his eyes telling him she knew he had sent her some money—money which he must now know she had never received.

He shrugged, 'I guess so,' he muttered, and gave her a searching look. 'Was it bad, girl? I'd never forgive myself if you was unhappy. Thought I was doing the right thing, see? Teacher said you were bright, and I knew you'd never get anywhere staying around here.' He gave her a look she well remembered from the old days. 'Bit too attached to the place, you were. I knew if I sent you to one of the state schools, you'd get back here somehow, even if it meant walking all the way. 'Sides,' he growled, ''tis no place to bring up a young lady. You needed a woman to make you mind your p's and q's, show you what's what, like.'

Josie looked away quickly, and studied the worn carpet on the floor. She knew her grandfather was right in what he had said about her being attached to Carella—but it was not so much the place as him—although he hadn't said so. He was also right about her running away from wherever he had sent her and homing it right back to him. She sighed softly. So he had made sure by sending her all those miles away.

'Was it bad, girl?' he asked, breaking into her musings.

Josie looked back at him swiftly, 'Not really,' she said with a sad smile. 'I suppose I had all I needed—except for affection,' and seeing his swift scowl at this brief but telling statement, she added hastily, 'But I did learn to mind my p's and q's. And what's more, I'm a qualified teacher.' Her eyes softened as she met the still searching ones of her grandfather. 'I owe it all to you, Gramps,' she said quietly. 'I know everything now—how you paid for my education—oh, and for everything! Now don't your dare deny it,' she said half-scoldingly. 'I saw those letters—I also saw her bank account,' she added fiercely, 'and I only wish I'd had the power to give most of that money back, but she made sure I wouldn't get it by willing it elsewhere.'

He said nothing for a moment or so, then growled half to himself, as if searching his memory, 'Had a photo of you. You must have been about fifteen. All dolled up you was, in riding kit. Newspaper photo. She sent me that, so I knew you was okay.' He shook his head. 'Didn't think ...'

Again Josie's eyes centred on the carpet, not wanting him to see the swift flash of anger these words produced. She knew which photo he was talking about, and could guess the reason he had been supplied with one. Her riding fees! Not that any were paid. She had had to work for what riding lessons she was given, doing the mucking out and endless grooming of the horses in the stable. As for the riding kit, it had been borrowed for that one occasion from the daughter of the owner of the stables who had gone down with a heavy cold, and Josie had been pulled into action to take her place in a pony team competing for county honours. Her aunt hadn't, Josie thought bitterly, missed a trick, and she wondered what else she had stung her grandfather for. She sighed inwardly; there was no point in telling the truth now, in any case, her grandfather had probably worked it out for himself; he was never slow to read between the lines.

Breaking in on her musings, he said slowly as his gaze went round the dusty room and faded furnishings, 'Guess it's not much of a home now, girl, but you're welcome, anyway.' A tiny silence followed, and then he cleared his throat. 'Had a bit of bad luck. Crops failed two years running, and that was that,' he said with a hint of an apology in his voice.

Josie swallowed convulsively. It would take more than a couple of years to bring things to this pass. Precisely twelve years, she thought miserably. How could he have let her aunt bleed him to bankruptcy? And it wasn't as if Josie could repay him, she had seen to that. She drew in a shuddering breath. There was so much she wanted to ask him, but wasn't sure how to go about it. 'I suppose Mr Muntrose has left?' she queried idly.

Her grandfather nodded abruptly. 'Had a family to keep. I had to push him out at that; no sense in keeping him on. My fault,' he said harshly, 'them sprinklers ought to have been replaced years ago, Dan mentioned it often enough. As it was, they packed up at a time when they were most needed, and that was that.'

Josie glanced up at him swiftly, hoping her sympathy did not show in her eyes. He was trying to tell her it was a case of bad management, but she knew better. The money was not there to replace the sprinkler system, so the business had collapsed.

'Guess it would have happened sooner or later,' he went on wearily. 'Not so young as I was. Dan was doing more than his share as it was. He's up at Blue Mount now. Got a good job, too.'

'Blue Mount?' echoed Josie, searching in her memory, but failing to identify the name.

'Kade Boston's place,' answered Joseph, a trifle drily. 'Course, you wouldn't remember the name, he came long after you left. Used to be Sam Laton's place. Boston bought it up about three years ago, and most of the land hereabouts.' He gave Josie a quick searching look as if wondering how much to tell her. 'Bought most of my land, too. No sense in hanging on to it. My working days were over.'

A sudden vision of a tall, hard man came into Josie's mind, and she wrinkled her nose when recalling the way he had spoken to her. 'Was that Kade Boston I met when I arrived?' she queried indignantly.

Her grandfather started, and on her next words relaxed slightly. 'He seemed a very rude man,' she complained, and looked at him. 'He wasn't in a very good mood, I gathered.'

Joseph West grinned and rubbed a hand over his chin. 'Guess he'd plenty to be sore about,' he replied, and then grew serious again. 'Think I might take him up on his offer, though.' he muttered. 'He's about right in what he said. 'Specially if you're set on staying,' he added, giving her an interrogative look.

Josie met his eyes squarely. 'Of course I'm staying!' she answered swiftly. 'But do you have to sell up, Gramps?' she asked pleadingly. 'Couldn't we keep the house, and some of the land? I can get a job, and keep us,' she added coaxingly, and her spirits dropped to zero as she saw his jaw tighten, and knew she had hurt that fierce pride of his.

When he spoke, however, she was immediately relieved of this conjecture, for he had not been listening to the latter part of her speech. 'So you heard, then?' he said harshly.

Josie nodded slowly. 'I couldn't help hearing,' she said softly. 'So you'd better tell me everything, hadn't you?' she added.

Her grandfather was quiet for a few seconds as if marshalling his thoughts, then he began with, 'Well, you heard what he said about his cattle.' He moved restlessly. 'Them fences want repairing.' He sighed. 'Guess they want more than repairing, replacing more likely.' He looked down at Josie and ruffled her hair. 'Well, if that's the way you want it, we might just be able to hold off selling— I'm not promising, mind you. It depends, like. Kade Boston ain't a patient man, and this isn't the first time he's complained.'

'He doesn't look a patient man,' Josie said dryly. 'But I gathered you'd already said no to his proposal, and that was why he was in such a temper.'

Joseph West gave a slow grin. 'Guess I was feeling ornery,' he replied. 'Knew I'd have to give in one day; didn't feel like obliging him at the time. As for that long stocking he thinks I'm hiding, he's in for a surprise if he tries to make me pay out for any lost stock—and he ain't the only one,' he added in a soft voice.

Josie heard but said nothing, and waited for him to go on, but he seemed tired of the subject, and changed it by demanding to know everything about her, where she had gone to school, and where she had qualified. The rest of that day was taken up by Josie filling in the gaps of the years.

The following morning, Josie awoke to a brilliantly sunny morning, and lay for a while planning her day. The most important item on the agenda was a job for herself. It had taken a little while for her grandfather to accept the fact that she intended to provide for him, and Josie had had to be very careful, not to mention tactful, in offering this intention. As she had told him, if she had still been in England, she would have had to work anyway, and what was the use of having a diploma if one never used it? This argument eventually won the day, but posed another problem, for the local school was small, and only required the services of one teacher, which it had, and according to her grandfather, was likely to have for some years to come, as the last teacher had recently retired, and a younger woman had taken over the appointment.

There must, thought Josie, be something else she could do. She had no intention of moving away to a larger town in order to obtain employment. She meant to stay near to her grandfather, come what may, and she couldn't look after him if she had to dash off each morning to catch a bus, and return late in the evening, for distances here were on a greater scale than at home, and the chance of her obtaining a teaching post in a nearby township was non-existent. A slight sigh escaped her on this thought; it would have been nice to have done the work she was trained for, but if it meant separation from her beloved Gramps, then it was out of the question.

As she dressed later, her mind went over the previous evening's conversation, and how her grandfather adroitly changed the subject each time it veered back to him, and what had happened to the market garden. Lack of money had played a big part in its collapse, but knowing her grandfather, Josie simply couldn't understand why he had let things get to this pass. He had always been a fighter, and in the old days would have welcomed the challenge, and would have somehow got back on top. She sighed as she left her room and went down to start the breakfast. He was old, of course, but even so, it didn't gell with what Josie knew of him; he had never been one to bow down to fate.

Within a few hours, she was given the answers to these vexing questions. Having taken an inventory of the contents of the larder, and finding it sadly lacking in even the barest essentials, she saw that her grandfather had lived mainly off tinned food, when he remembered to feed himself, and that, Josie suspected, was not on a regular basis. This state of affairs she intended to put straight right away, and was grateful that she had some money by her, that would enable her to purchase what she required.

When she had washed up the breakfast dishes, she sat down and compiled a list of her require-ments, and after calling out to her grandfather, who had settled himself on the back porch, that she wouldn't be long, she set off for the town.

A tiny smile played round her lips as she left the house, recalling her grandfather's anxious query as to whether she remembered the way. In his eyes she was still a small girl, she thought, but she had sensed an underlying worry of his that she might not return, and at this thought her smile faded. It had taken him some time to realise that she was back, and meant to stay, and he had been pathetic-ally pleased to see her at breakfast, although he had done his best to hide this fact from her, and had been a little on the grumpy side, but Josie hadn't been fooled by this camouflage.

As she entered the town her mind was busy making plans of what she considered priority jobs. The weeds, for one thing, would have to be cleared, not only from the front of the house, but the back, too. She frowned as she recalled Kade Boston's furious remarks about his cattle and the likelihood of them being poisoned by them. Her lips set in a firm line. Well, that made the back of the house the first priority. Then there was the fencing to be seen to—providing it was in a fit state to be repaired, and this Josie doubted very much. She sighed. How much was fencing, anyway? and how much land did her grandfather still own? There were so many questions to be answered, and so much to be done, and all to be accomplished without upsetting that fierce pride of his.

The first store Josie came to was the candy store, and she felt a wave of nostalgia as she looked through the small archway that led to the shop, and wondered if dour old Mr Hobson was there, and if so, would he still recognise her? She frowned on trying to recall just how old he had been, for at the age of ten she had thought him very old, but he might only have been in his thirties. One was apt to look on anyone above twenty as in their dotage at that tender age, she mused smilingly.

Her thoughts were abruptly curtailed as she caught sight of a small card glued to the glass door of the store, that stated that help was required, and would anyone interested enquire within. A sparkle came into Josie's eyes; she wanted a job, didn't she? She pushed open the door and went inside.

The shop was empty when she entered, and while she waited for someone to attend to her, her eyes swept round the store. There had been some changes, she noticed. For one thing, more space had been made, and her eyes rested on a separate counter at the end of the store, above which hung a sign that read 'Soda fountain', where presumably soft drinks were served, and milk shakes were made up. Josie did not remember such a service before, and she seemed to remember that there had once been shelves there.

A man appeared from a door behind the area she was staring at, and Josie's eyes widened in disbelief. It couldn't be—could it? She waited until he had finished the task of wiping the counter down and looked up to serve her.

'Nat?' Josie asked a little uncertainly.

Nat Muntrose started, and stared at her. His slight frown told Josie he was trying to place her. She smiled at him. 'Well, I knew you,' she said delightedly. 'Don't tell me I've changed that much!'

'Josie?' he asked in half belief, making her smile widen at his incredulity.

'I'll have two sticks of liquorice,' she said grandly, 'and you can have one if you give me some of your lemon drops.'

Nat grinned, and came from behind the counter with hand outstretched towards her. 'Now I know it's you,' he said with a chuckle. 'What in tarnation have you been doing all these years?'.

'First things first,' answered Josie, accepting the proffered hand, and thinking that for all his height, he was just the same Nat she had known all that time ago. He was still very thin, and still had that gawky way of walking that she remembered so well. 'Has the job gone?' she asked quickly.

Nat's eyes widened at the question and he gave her a questioning look. 'You mean ...' he began slowly, not sure whether to finish the sentence or not.

Josie nodded. 'Yes. I want it. Are you working here, or do you own the store?' she queried.

He grinned. 'Reckon I'd paid for it with all the candies I used to buy,' he told her, then reverted back to Josie's previous request and scratched his head. 'You sure you want the job?' he asked.

'Absolutely certain,' returned Josie seriously. 'I'm back to stay, and I shall need something to do to keep me occupied.'

There was something in her voice that caught Nat's attention. She hadn't, he thought, changed all that much. Of course she looked different, as well she might after twelve years; grown into quite a beauty, he thought, and wondered why she hadn't been snapped up in the marriage mart. His gaze lingered on her hands. No rings were in evidence, so presumably she was still single, and he thought that the Englishmen must be very slow on the uptake to allow such a state of affairs. As for needing a job—and she meant it, he knew this; his lips thinned as the thought that the old man had clammed up on her too went through his mind. Shaking these thoughts off, he met her anxious gaze and gave a grin. 'Sure. Okay, it's yours. We don't pay a fortune, mind you, and I guess the wife will want a say in it, too.' His grin widened. 'Guess it depends if she'll forgive you for pulling her pigtails when you sat behind her in class.'

Josie's eyes widened. 'Lucy Hobson?' she exclaimed, then gave a comical half grimace. 'Well, that settles it! I shall be turned down out of hand,' she added mournfully.

Nat chuckled. 'Not if I know my girl, you won't. She'll be too busy catching up on the years between the pair of you, and parading our family. To hear her talk we've the brightest kids this side of

the universe,' he frowned slightly as a thought
struck him. 'Well, you can't win 'em all. Our
Billy's a bit on the slow side—has trouble with
reading. Teacher called it some fancy name, I can't
rightly recall right now, but the others are bright
enough.'

Josie looked interested. 'A sort of word blind-
ness?' she asked.

Nat gave a surprised start. 'Sure—I guess that's
what she meant.'

'Is that why you asked for help?' queried Josie.
'With his reading, I mean?'

Nat shook his head. 'Nope—though he sure
needs help.' He nodded towards the soda fountain.
'That's the job we had in mind. Lucy took it on
for a spell, but what with the kids, she found it
hard going.' He gave Josie another doubtful look.
'As I said, we can't pay much. Lucy's dad kinda let
things slip, and we're only just showing a profit.'

Josie smiled back reassuringly. 'I still want the
job,' she said gently. 'I want to help pay my way,
Nat, and,' she added brightly, 'I'll give your Billy
some private coaching lessons into the bargain.
What do you say?'

His eyes widened as he replied slowly. 'Well,
that's just what the teacher said he'd need, but that
sort of help is hard to come by. Lucy tries, but she
still gives a hand in the shop when we have a busy
spell.' He frowned. 'I know it worries her, though,
that she can't spend as much time on him as she'd
like, not with three other youngsters to keep an
eye on.'

'Well,' replied Josie grandly, reminding Nat of
the young Josie, 'I shall give him the benefit of my

four-year training course, until, that is, I accept an appointment to some university.' Her twinkling eyes belied this grand statement, but Nat was suitably impressed.

'You're a teacher?' he exclaimed in wonderment, then looked towards the soda fountain and shook his head slowly. 'You ought to be able to do better than that,' he half muttered, but Josie heard him.

'I know, Nat, and eventually I will,' she replied seriously. 'But right now I need a start,' she shrugged. 'Something to be going on with. It doesn't matter what,' she added.

Nat nodded understandingly, and with a grin asked her if she would care for a coffee. It was about time he had one, he said, and in any case he couldn't let her go without seeing Lucy, and she ought to be in shortly, after taking the kids to school. 'Course,' he added as he led the way through a door that led to their private quarters, 'she has to catch up on the gossip while she's about it. Good job we're never busy at this time in the morning, or it would be just too bad!'

Josie sat in the small but comfortable living room while Nat fixed the coffee in the kitchen, giving her snatches of gossip as he worked, although most of it was meaningless to Josie, she had been away too long, but she was interested in Nat's family. He mentioned the fact that his father was now working for Kade Boston, and this Josie already knew, but she said nothing. 'That rancher sure livened the town up,' he remarked as he carried the cups through to the living-room. 'And I guess it needed it,' he frowned. 'What with other businesses folding up, he just about injected the life-saver. Oh, sure, lots of townsfolk kinda resented his high and mighty way of taking over—at first, that was, until they found out he was a big man in his trade and that brought trade to this place. There's talk of a hotel being built to accommodate buyers that drop in on spec to take a look at his stock; and going by the mighty fancy prices they pay for his cattle, I guess they're pretty fine stock.' He handed Josie her coffee. 'I never thought Dad would settle down there, but seems he's got a good job in their records office, and though he misses the outdoor life, he's happy enough.'

Accepting the coffee, Josie smiled her thanks and thought about Nat's father. In missing the outdoor life, Nat was referring to the job he had had with her grandfather, and she was in no doubt that the 'businesses folding up' reference applied solely to the market garden, for once upon a time her grandfather had been the 'big man' around those parts.

As if sensing her thoughts, Nat said as he settled himself in the chair opposite her, 'He sure changed.'

Josie didn't have to ask whom he was talking about, but just waited for him to go on, and he did, saying abruptly: 'Dad couldn't get through to him at all,' and giving her a mournful look continued, 'Weren't all that long after you went to the U.K. He just clammed up on everyone—thought he was missing you—least, Dad thought so; but each time he said anything about you he got his head bitten off.' He gave a grin, then sobered.

'Sprinklers packed up soon afterwards, and that was that. Dad tried to get him to see sense and pay out for new equipment.'

He drank some of his coffee, then went on, 'Stands to reason he could afford it, but it seems he'd just lost interest, and things went from bad to worse. Dad stuck it out as long as he could—as it was, I think it was old Joseph that pushed him out—he'd got a family to look out for.' He put his cup down and searched for a packet of cigarettes, and offering Josie one, that she refused, continued: 'It did cross our minds that something had happened to you.' He gave her a searching look. 'Thought the world of you, he did, but whatever it was, he wouldn't let on—no way.' He drew on his cigarette and expelled it in a long plume of smoke. 'After a while folk stopped asking questions and let him get on with it. No sense in sticking your neck out for chopping—which was what they got when they approached him.' He stared at the end of his cigarette. 'Seems he turned miser as well; used to be a good spender in the town—well, you know how he used to be—he never gave you candy money without making sure us kids had something too,' he remarked, giving Josie a quick look.

She nodded and her eyes turned misty. Gramps had let everybody think he was hoarding money, when all the time he was sending every available cent to her—or thought he was. For him to be so short of money so soon after her departure, it looked as if the woman who had agreed to take her—Josie simply couldn't think of her as 'Aunt', not now—had demanded a lump sum to start with. Waiting until Josie was with her, and then making the demand. She sighed inwardly; it was hardly something her grandfather could explain, was it? that he was being subtly blackmailed by a member of his own family. Even though the relationship was only by marriage, it didn't make it any more acceptable. She swallowed and asked Nat quickly, 'Nat, do you think he's got a long stocking, as everybody else seems to think?'

He gave her a gloomy look and shrugged as he stubbed out his cigarette in the tray on the table. 'Guess he must have,' he answered slowly. 'He doesn't spend much, and it's common knowledge he must have made a packet out of selling off part of his land to Kade Boston.'

Putting her coffee cup down on the table, Josie looked back at Nat who was studying his feet. 'What if I told you he was broke, Nat?' she said quietly, and nodded in affirmation as his startled eyes met hers. 'He's been paying for my education,' she went on, still in that quiet voice. 'And broke himself doing it.'

She pushed back a strand of hair that had clung to her cheek, with an impatient gesture. The ins and outs didn't matter at this time—or the fact that she hadn't received a quarter of what had been sent, she just wanted people to know how it was. Only too well could she imagine her grandfather's hurt and stubborn pride that had made him hold his tongue, not even confiding in Dan Muntrose, who had been more than an employee to him, for if he had, Josie was sure Dan would have found a way of explaining the circumstances to others, without causing embarrassment to her grandfather; and what was more important, would have made sure he was still respected by the town folk. As it was, they had avoided him, and dubbed him a miser in the process. Her hands clenched into small fists; well, they would soon know the truth, she would make certain of that! She looked back at Nat, who seemed to be having trouble in digesting her last statement, and gave an offhanded shrug. 'If only I'd known,' she said casually. 'But I didn't dream things were so costly,' and quickly looked down at the floor as she saw Nat's quick surprised glance at her. 'So the least I can do is try and make up for it now,' she said firmly, adding as her eyes met Nat's, 'I'm a modern version of the Prodigal Son, Nat!'

Nat stared at her suspiciously, and after a moment's thought remarked, 'Well, that don't sound like the Josie I used to know. Can't see you draining the old man of his last penny.' He shot her a long considering look. 'Seems like you changed too.'

'Oh, I did,' Josie got out quickly, not giving him time to think things out. 'I told you I didn't know how things were,' she gave him a bright challenging look. 'I didn't even bother to write,' she added for good measure, and gave a sigh. 'I think I never forgave him for sending me away like that. I suppose I looked on it as conscience money.'

Nat was plainly puzzled and showed it by scratching his head. A tiny silence followed, then he said half to himself, 'Could be. You were mighty put out at going, if I recall,' then he added in a low voice, 'Folk are going to feel pretty bad over this if it comes out.'

Josie said nothing, but waited for him to go on.

'It might be as well if things are left as they are,' he told her after giving her a considering look. 'But I'd like to tell my dad, if you'll let me. He thought a lot of your granddad, and it'll clear up a few things that didn't make sense at the time. But that's as far as it will go. No call for others to know, they'll only put the wrong construction on things anyway.'

'That's not the way I want it done,' answered Josie with a note of determination in her voice. 'I want everyone to know. I don't care about myself, but I do care about Gramps. The sooner everybody knows there's no long stocking, the better. And,' she added fiercely, 'I won't have everyone thinking of him as a miser and shunning him as if he were a leper, do you hear? I want the truth to come out, and I'm depending on you to pass on the news.'

Her vehemence convinced Nat that she meant every word, but he wasn't happy about it. 'Folk can be mighty unkind,' he warned her. 'Might make things difficult for you.' He screwed his eyes up in thought. 'Might even think you've come back to collect on what's left before he hands in his dinner pail.'

Josie's eyes met his squarely as she asked quietly, 'Is that what you think, Nat?'

A slow shake of the head gave her the answer before he spoke. 'Nope,' he said firmly. 'I believe you; you couldn't have known how things were— as you said—and it's like the old man to keep quiet about it.' He gave her a grin. 'And it's like you to try and make up for it. I haven't forgotten the day you gave all your candy money to a kid that hadn't got a dad to look out for him.' He sighed on his next thought. 'Okay,' he said abruptly, 'I'll do as you say, but remember what I said about small-minded town folk.'

Josie let out a small sigh of relief; Nat would keep his word and pass the news along, she also knew he would do his best to protect her from the kind of gossip that was certain to spring from such information, but she felt reasonably certain that none of it would ever affect her seriously in the future. However, time was to tell a different story.

CHAPTER THREE

Nat's forecast of his wife's reaction to the news that Josie was not only back in the fold, but was going to work for them, proved unerringly correct, and Josie soon found herself caught up in the whirl of the Muntroses' family life.

True to her word, she managed to fit in at least an hour each day with Billy, painstakingly going over previous school work that he had failed to grasp because of his handicap, and during this time Lucy would take her place at the soda fountain. It was an admirable arrangement on both sides, and had Lucy had her way, Billy would have been kept away from school, and Josie take over his entire schooling. However, Nat had something to say about that, and Josie had to agree that he was right, for Billy needed to be kept with the other children. To treat him differently would be to highlight his difficulties. Done this way, it was looked upon simply as extra schooling and would cause no embarrassment to the child.

Josie's worry over the way her grandfather might take the news that she had found a job in the township, doing what he could well describe as work beneath her capabilities, was pleasantly allayed by his abrupt nod, and his calm acceptance of the fact that she would have to wait a while until a better opportunity presented itself. It seemed to Josie that he was willing to bow that fierce pride of his aside, allowing nothing to come between them that might tempt her to go away again.

Before long Josie had the house straight, if not back to its previous splendour, for curtains needed replacing, and the carpets were on the threadbare borders. Not that any of these things bothered Josie, for the washing of curtains and the polishing of furniture had made it a home again, not the shell of a dwelling she had walked into a short while before.

The garden, too, came under fire from her busy fingers, and the weeds were ruthlessly torn up and piled in a heap for burning. This work was confined to the evenings, but she had to be careful not to overdo the amount of time she spent on these chores, working them in while her grandfather snoozed on the back porch, and timing her return to the house when she judged he would be ready for company. If she was tired, and there were many evenings she could cheerfully have gone straight to her room and collapsed on the bed, she successfully hid this fact from him. The satisfaction of putting all in order again drove her on relentlessly.

By the time two weeks had passed, Josie had broken the back of the work needed to be done on the front and back gardens, and had been able to turn her attention to the outer fringes of what was left of her grandfather's property, and as she surveyed the rotting fences and open spaces caused by the collapse of the fences, she could well see Kade Boston's point. Those fences would have to be seen to, although most would have to be replaced, she thought as her fingers touched the rotting wood of one section.

Her forehead creased as she tried to assess the amount of fencing required, but she gave up the struggle after a while. She would have to ask Nat for help on that one. It was no use asking her grandfather, for before she knew it he would be tackling the job himself, if only to prove that he was still capable of such work, but he was not, for Josie had not missed the fact that he got breathless extremely quickly, and she meant to get the doctor to give him a check-up when she could persuade him to seek medical aid. So much had already been accomplished since her return that she saw no difficulty in getting her way in this matter, if she chose the right time to bring the subject up.

The fact had gradually been borne in on her that it was her supposed desertion of him that had been the prime factor in his enforced way of life. Bitterness in seeing his life's work slowly edging to a standstill through lack of funds, coupled with the fact that he was being held to ransom, was hard enough to take, without the added sorrow of an uncaring granddaughter.

As Josie was slowly straightening out the house and the surrounding land, so too was her grandfather's life changing. Meal times were prompt, and no waiting until he needed to eat. Canned meals were a thing of the past for him—Josie saw to that, for her stay in lodgings while she was at college had taught her how to cook, for there had been no extra money to pay for such luxuries as having her meals cooked for her, as some of the other more well-endowed students had had. It had been a case of subsisting on the grant she had obtained, and when that had dried up, finding an evening job to keep her going until the next cheque arrived.

Although it had been hard, Josie was now grateful for the lessons learnt on how to survive on the barest amount of money available, for had she received what she should have received from her grandfather, she would have been featherbedded right through college, and would now have been flummoxed on how she could possibly feed not only herself, but her grandfather also, on the small wage she earned each week at the soda fountain. Although it was not so small as she had at first imagined, going by Nat's apologetic air when he mentioned the amount, and she had in fact been pleasantly surprised. Yes, she could manage, and was happy to do so.

Apart from the curiosity aroused by Josie's return, shown by the sudden inrush of folk to buy anything from candy to ice cream, giving them an excuse to take a good look at the newcomer in their midst, there was no sign of their attitude towards her grandfather changing, and this worried Josie, for she knew Nat had complied with her request. She could hardly have been ignorant of this, for although curiosity was there, there had been no friendly overtures from the people Nat had introduced her to. That they saw her as a modern version of 'Diamond Lil' was only too plain, and she could sense their disappointment in finding her dressed in a cheap cotton dress, much as the women wore themselves, and Josie felt that she ought at least to sport a diamond bracelet to live up to the part.

Eventually the day arrived when she returned home to find her grandfather scowling over a letter he had received that morning, and passing it over to her with a curt, 'Must be getting short of respectable citizens,' he left her to peruse the contents.

It was an invitation for her grandfather to sit on the town's welfare committee, and Josie's heart sang as she read the polite, almost pleading missive. It was their way of saying sorry, she was sure of it. She looked back at her grandfather, who was pretending he was busy filling his pipe, but she knew he was waiting for her comments. If he had read that invitation once, he had read it a dozen times, Josie thought, judging by the several creases made where it had been folded and unfolded.

Managing to instil some indignation into her voice, Josie said quickly, 'Well, they've got a nerve! How can you be expected to sit on a committee? I mean, surely they've got some younger folk they can ask? No, Gramps, you turn them down, you've done your share for the town. It's time you took things easy.'

To her hastily concealed delight, he jumped on the oblique challenge with a growled, 'Just you hold on a moment. I'm not ready to be put out to graze yet.' He was silent for a moment or so, then he said, 'Been wondering just how long Kade Boston would run things around here. Guessed he'd taken more on his plate than he could handle.' He rubbed his chin, a sign that told Josie that he would accept the invitation. He always did that when he had some scheme in mind, and his next words proved it. 'Guess there are a few things I'd like to bring up.' He gave her a fierce glare. 'Folk thought I'd buried my head in the sand these past few years, so it's about time I put them right on that for a start.' He nodded to himself. 'About time some of them came calling too, so you can get acquainted.'

This was not exactly what Josie had in mind, but she was content enough that the first steps had been taken. to embroil her grandfather in the affairs of the town again, but woe betide anyone who spoke disparagingly of his granddaughter! She could see squalls ahead if he caught even the slightest hint of such gossip, but it was a chance she had had to take, telling herself that it would be a very brave man, or woman, come to that, who left themselves wide open to Joseph West's fire, and were sure to tread warily in this direction.

Now that her main objective had been reached, Josie gave her attention to other matters. The fencing being the more pressing item on the agenda, she put the question to Nat the following day. It did not occur to her at the time to mention the specific reason why she needed the fencing so urgently, and Nat had assumed it was wanted to fence off certain areas of the garden, with the result of a delivery a few days later of a goodly amount of definitely inferior fencing left outside the house for Josie's inspection.

Her first reaction was to make arrangements to have it returned. It was absolutely hopeless for the task she had in mind, she thought, as her blue eyes gazed bleakly at the weathered and worm-eaten staking. No wonder she had got it so cheaply, she thought miserably. Why, it was in no better condition than the fencing she had wanted to replace.

However, a small incident later that evening caused her to change her mind, and even be grateful for any sort of fencing, inferior, or otherwise! She had wandered down to the edge of the property with the intention of seeing whether there was any hope of salvaging parts of the fence that had either been trampled down by cattle that had strayed over the boundary, or had simply collapsed through neglect, when she came across a young steer foraging around what had once been a vegetable garden. Picking up a stick and uttering a few bloodcurdling yells, she drove it back to the other side of the boundary, taking particular note of the gap it made for in its flight out of the vicinity.

Keeping a cautious eye out for any further strays, she found that it had apparently wandered off from the herd, for she saw no sign of the rest of the herd and fervently thanked providence for this, for she doubted whether she could have handled the situation on her own.

As she watched the young steer disappearing over a ridge in the distance, her brooding eyes came back to the gap. It had headed automatically through that section, and that meant it had been there before, and judging by the churned-up soil, so had a few more. Her glance strayed along the boundary line and she noted that though there were several gaps in the dilapidated fencing, the gap in front of her was by far the worst and required immediate attention.

Deciding that any kind of fencing was better

than none, Josie headed back to the front of the house where she had left the fencing delivered earlier, and hoping the notes her grandfather had started to make in preparation for his debut on the town committee were still keeping him occupied, she ferreted out an old wheelbarrow, and piling as many stakes as she could safely transport in one journey, she made the cumbersome passage back to the boundary line.

Having successfully managed that part of the operation, it was a little disconcerting to find that she had forgotten a few but vitally important items, such as a heavy duty hammer to knock the stakes in place with, not to mention some form of wire or twine to lock them together. Josie could have wept with frustration at such foolishness on her part. She just wasn't thinking straight; couldn't have been, to have even imagined she could manage such a task on her own.

However, it wasn't long before the streak of obstinacy she had inherited from Joseph West took control, and she refused to be beaten. She had got so far, and simply would not give up now. With a determination bordering on desperation, she made the return journey to search out the items she required. The hammer, she was sure, was some-where in the house, and she vaguely remembered coming across it on one of her tidying up spurts earlier on; she had tucked it away in the box of tools in the packing room just off the back porch. And there just might, she told herself, be a few more things in that room that would come in handy—such as the twine that used to be tied round the boxes of produce when the market garden sold vegetables to the neighbouring farms and town stores.

On these thoughts her heart lifted out of its despondency; all wasn't lost yet. It all depended on how much time she had left before her grandfather demanded to know what was keeping her so busy. Her fears on this score were soon allayed by his recumbent form as he lay asleep in his old rocking chair on the porch, one hand still clutching the paper he had started to make notes on.

Josie smiled as she passed him; it was probably the first sleep he had had that day. The letter would have kept his mind busy during the day, in which case she would have all the time she required for the task in hand, she told herself, as she entered the old storeroom.

Collecting the hammer, she looked around for some of the twine she had hoped to find, and was rewarded shortly by finding a complete spool. Her fingers touched the strong cording; strong enough to do the job, she told herself happily, and a fence was a fence. The cattle would see a barrier, and that would be good enough to keep them out. They were not likely to examine it for weak structure, or note that the staking was worm-eaten.

Armed with the necessary tools, this time remembering all she would need to complete the job, including a knife to cut the twine when needed, Josie made the final trip out to the boundary. The work proved not quite so hard as she had envisaged, for she was able to replace the fencing without a great deal of physical exertion by sinking the stakes in the holes left by the previous fencing, hammering them in without too much bother.

When the gap had been closed, she interlocked each stake with the twine, and when she had finished she stood back to admire her handiwork. With her head on one side and her eyes slightly narrowed, she nodded to herself. It wasn't what one might call perfect, but it would do the job until she could make other arrangements, and next time, she told herself, she would make certain Nat knew just what she needed the fencing for—perhaps he would also know of someone who would do the job for her when she had saved enough money to buy good fencing. On this thought she gave a sigh; if what she had paid out for the stakes was anything to go by, it was going to be a long time before she could afford to buy the wood, let alone pay someone to put it up for her.

It was dusk by the time Josie returned to the house, and she was in dire need of a shower, and was now beginning to feel the effects of her labour. In all she had had to make three trips out with the fencing on the wheelbarrow, and the ache she felt across her shoulders was due to the unaccustomed exercise of not only pushing a loaded barrow, but the hammering in of the stakes.

Her grandfather awoke just as she passed the porch and sat up abruptly, then looked down at the paper in his hand, trying to pretend that he had been studying it for some time. 'Guess I've not been much company tonight,' he said a little apologetically to Josie, adding a shade defiantly, 'Got a lot of things I want to bring up at that meeting.'

In spite of her tiredness Josie had to grin at this

little white lie of his to preserve his dignity. 'Of course, Gramps,' she said with a twinkle in her eye. 'And I took the opportunity to do a little gardening. What I need now is a cool shower, so I'll leave you to get on with your notes,' and she left him staring after her with a suspicion of an answering twinkle in his eyes.

The following morning she told Nat about the invitation her grandfather had received from the town committee, adding with a smile, 'He was tickled pink—although he would have hated me to know it. I was only afraid he'd turn it down flat, so I advised him to do just that.' Her smile widened to a grin. 'He rose to the bait beautifully!'

Nat grinned back at her. 'You haven't forgotten how to handle him, then?' he said teasingly. 'You could always twist him round your little finger, if I recall rightly.'

'It's because I'm so like him,' answered Josie, then her expression sobered as she thought of all the wasted years between them. She ought to have known he wouldn't push her out of his life as her aunt had intimated that he had, and he ought to have known better than to think she had changed that much.

Her expression gave Nat an inkling of her thoughts, and his glance sharpened as he asked, 'There's more to that story than you've told me, isn't there?'

Josie's blue eyes rested thoughtfully on the serving counter in front of her. 'It doesn't matter now, Nat,' she said quietly. 'The thing is, everything's turned out right.' Her voice grew fierce as she added, 'And that's just how it ought to be.'

Nat sighed, and turned his attention to replacing the empty sweet jars with full ones. 'Guess you'll tell me when you're good and ready,' he said sadly.

Two evenings later Josie slipped down to the boundary to see if her fence was still intact, and long before she reached the boundary line she stood blinking in astonishment at the sight that met her incredulous eyes. Of her tireless efforts two nights ago there was no sign—but there was indeed fencing there, and her bemused eyes took in the staunch six-foot wired stakes—strong enough, she presumed, to withstand a herd charging at full gallop!

Her eye then caught the remnants of her puny efforts. The worn stakes had been pulled out of the ground and just flung down by the side of that impressive barrier, making it look even more innocuous than it really was. Her glance went back to the fence, and she saw that not only had the original gap been covered, but the whole of the boundary line as far as she could see. Her breath expelled slowly as she thought of the cost of the operation, and she wondered if her grandfather had come to some arrangement with Kade Boston—had he sold him more land? On this thought her hands clenched by her side. Had Kade Boston been back to bully him when she was at the store? There was only one way to find out, and Josie turned on her heel and marched back to the house.

She arrived back just in time to help her grandfather win the battle over the bow tie he was tussling with in his preparations for his appearance on the committee that evening. 'Gramps?' she demanded as she gave the tie a final tweak into position. 'Have you sold some more land to Kade Boston?'

He straightened his cuffs before he replied indignantly, 'Said I wouldn't, didn't I?' and gave her a suspicious stare. 'Why?' he barked.

Josie swallowed and wished she had held her tongue. If she wasn't careful he would find out about her attempts to fill that gap in the boundary. 'Oh, well,' she said, managing to sound casual about it, 'there's a brand new fence up now that covers the whole boundary—a pretty formidable one, too,' she added idly, 'and I just thought ...' She left the rest of the sentence unsaid.

Joseph gave the matter some thought, then to her amazement grinned. 'So he got tired of waiting for me to dig in that long stocking he thinks I have, did he? Well, that's up to him. Now if I'd made my own arrangements and it hadn't suited his purpose—well, that would be a different kettle of fish—as it is, he's taken the matter into his own hands and he'll have to foot the bill. I'm not complaining.'

Josie gulped; did that mean that her grandfather would have to pay the bill if the fencing already there was unsuitable? For it certainly had been, that much was obvious by the way it had been thrown aside as so much rubbish, she thought, as she recalled where it had been left. 'You mean he didn't say anything about what he was going to do?' she persisted, trying to stem the ghastly implication of what the result of her enforced labour was about to bring on her unsuspecting grand-father's head.

He calmly brushed a small crease out of his jacket pocket as he said, 'Kade Boston don't ask, child—he does!' His eyes blazed for a moment, then he half shrugged. 'As I said, I've no complaint on that score, not now. Had it been the old days, then things might have been different. He'd have met his match then—yes, sir!' He met Josie's eyes. 'Them days are gone, girl. From now on I sit back and let others do the fighting.'

He sounded almost regretful, Josie thought, but she grinned back at him affectionately. 'I'd love to be a fly on the wall at that meeting,' she told him teasingly. 'I'm sure a few folk will have a different point of view by the time the meeting is ad-journed!'

Old Joseph squared his bony shoulders, but his eyes held the familiar twinkle as he answered solemnly, 'Now who said I was going to cause a rumpus? I'm just going to bring up a few points that might have escaped their notice,' he pointed out reasonably.

The hooting of a horn broke up this happy dal-liance, and Josie walked to the door with him and had a word with Dan Muntrose, who had offered to collect his old boss and take him to the meeting.

As she waved them off, Josie felt very grateful for Dan's quick arrival back on the scene. It seemed he only wanted an excuse to be of some help to Joseph West, for she had since found out that though he had attempted in the past to keep in contact with her grandfather, Joseph's attitude towards his visits had hardly encouraged any such leanings. It was pride, of course, Josie thought sadly. He had wanted nothing to do with the past, and Dan had belonged to that past, even though he was the closest thing to a friend Joseph had ever had, and when Nat had told her later that his father was also on the committee, Josie was sure the invitation had been sent at his instigation.

Josie's pleasure at seeing her grandfather once more taking an interest in the town's welfare faded a short while later as she busied herself by ironing a few clothes she had washed before leaving for work that morning, and her thoughts inevitably turned towards Kade Boston and his presumptuous act in putting up that fence without so much as a 'May I?' It was still her grandfather's land when all was said and done—not, she thought, as she carefully folded one of her grandfather's shirts after she had pressed it, that it wasn't a great relief to know there would be no further trouble with strays in the future, but it was still an impertinent act on Kade's part. She frowned as she recalled her grandfather's words. Surely he would not have to foot the bill? The fencing of the property was his right, wasn't it? Her frown deepened; had he meant there would have been trouble if he had erected a fence and Kade Boston had replaced it? She nodded silently to herself at this thought; that must be it. Her grandfather might be old, but he had plenty of that old pride left, and she couldn't see him simply standing by and accepting such a happening. She sighed; if it had indeed been his fencing, then it would have been worthy of the name, not that pitiful barrier she had put up.

Her depression deepened as she thought of the

scathing remarks Kade Boston would be likely to make on her efforts should a confrontation take place. She put the iron down on the board with an abrupt movement as she imagined her grandfather's chagrin at being placed in such a position, and it was all her fault! Very likely he would go into a decline again, and all her hopes would be dashed. Why hadn't the wretched man let well alone? In time she would have replaced the fence herself. The more Josie thought about this, the more infuriated she became. Kade Boston might own most of the land thereabouts, but what right had he to impose his stamp on the last acre her grandfather had left, simply because he had money and they did not?

One thing stood out clearly, If Josie hoped to avoid a confrontation between her grandfather and Kade Boston over the fencing, she had to see Kade Boston and take full responsibility for the inadequate fencing that had been put up, and make quite certain that he understood the fact that her grandfather knew nothing of her efforts, and if he had any remarks to make on that score would he direct them at her!

CHAPTER FOUR

THE following morning the matter was still on Josie's mind, in spite of her grandfather's ruminations of the evening before. when he had returned from the meeting, tired but well satisfied with the outcome. One little item of news had temporarily dismissed the matter of the fencing from her mind, and that was that a new school was being built. It was something, her grandfather had told her, that had badly been needed for quite some time, and at last they had got down to the job, and they weren't doing things by half either. It was going to be a fine school, he said, and had given Josie a triumphant look. 'Looks as if you won't be too long at that job of yours,' he had said. 'They'll need more than one teacher, a place that size,' he had added happily.

He appeared to be quite certain that Josie had only to apply for a job there and that would be that, but Josie had her doubts. This was not England, and exception might be taken if she was given preference over others, for although she was American, she had been trained in England, and that was one factor her grandfather had not taken into consideration. Josie decided not to mention her thoughts on the matter; time enough for that when the school was nearing completion and staff were being sought.

Having dismissed the new school from her mind, she was back to the vexing problem of the fencing, and as she left the house to go to work, she wished fervently that for once the postboy would be early, to give her a chance to peruse the mail before it was put in the letter box. But he was not, and she just had to trust to luck that Kade Boston would not be prompt in either delivering a bill, or stating his reasons for fencing the boundary. There was, she thought miserably, nothing to stop him from going to see her grandfather, and should he do so there was nothing Josie could do about it, only hope he was kept exceptionally busy somewhere else and thus prevented from carrying out any such intention!

A few idle-sounding questions put by Josie that morning to Lucy, who was standing in for Nat while he visited the wholesalers for restocking his shelves, elicited the fact that Kade Boston rarely visited the township, but sent one of his men for whatever was required. He was, confided the gullible Lucy, a very important man, and on putting the question of, 'Had Josie seen him?', and receiving an affirmative nod, she rushed on with, 'Don't you think he's handsome? Set the single girls scheming, I can tell you, when he made his first appearance in the town.'

Josie was still thinking of Lucy's news that Kade Boston rarely came to town, and she wondered how she could get to see him, for she could not envisage herself going out to his ranch—not unless there was no other way of contacting him, so she only half listened to Lucy's rambling.

'Either that man's been let down, or he's a born bachelor,' went on Lucy, blithely unaware of Josie's preoccupation on an entirely different subject. 'Folk say he's too proud to take a fall over a woman,' she sighed. 'A real waste, I call it, but one thing's for sure—he doesn't take too kindly to feminine wiles.'

Josie came out of her musings in time to catch the bit about Kade Boston being too proud to fall for a woman—too hard, more likely, she thought, remembering those cold grey eyes of his. 'Not proud, Lucy,' she said, before she could stop herself, 'I'd say too hard.'

Lucy blinked and stared at her curiously; Josie sighed as she realised she would have to explain that statement. 'I arrived home in time to hear him go for Gramps over the gaps in the fencing.'

Her curiosity satisfied, Lucy confided, 'Well, he is a business man, Josie, and they say he's got a tongue like a whiplash when he's a mind to use it.' She gave Josie a grin. 'You know what? In lots of ways, what I hear tell of Kade Boston, he's a bit like your grandfather used to be—doesn't suffer fools gladly, as someone once put it.' Her eyes settled on a sweet jar that was slightly out of position, and she straightened it. 'I've only been in his company once,' she continued, looking back at Josie, who was having trouble finding a likeness between Kade Boston and her beloved grandfather, 'well, me and a hundred others,' she conceded with a grin. 'It wasn't long after he came to take over Blue Mount—leastways, it wasn't called Blue Mount in those days, but that's what he called it—anyway, the townsfolk thought they ought to make an effort to get acquainted with him, and held a social evening at the town hall, inviting him as guest of honour.' She thought for a

moment or two, then asked Josie, 'You don't remember Jessica Hanway, do you? I've a feeling
they came soon after you'd left; well, her father's
the mayor now, and as he's a widower that makes
Jessica the first lady—or whatever they're called—
she has to act hostess at all the official functions.
Not that we have that many occasions—in fact,'
she added thoughtfully, 'I wouldn't have thought
the town was big enough to warrant a mayor at all.
Still, they decided to elect one, and as Mr Hanway
owned the biggest store in town, the drug store, he
was given the job.'

She shook her head impatiently. 'I'm going off
the track again, as Nat would say,' she smiled at
Josie. 'What I was going to tell you was that Jessica
made a dead set at Kade Boston at that social.
Honestly, Josie, I'd have been ashamed to make
such a spectacle of myself as she did that night. She
might be what's considered a beauty,' she wrinkled
her nose slightly, 'if you go for the dark sultry
type, that is. I don't—besides, I've a personal
grudge against her; a friend of mine got badly hurt
when she played around with her fiancé—and I
mean played around. Jessica had no intention of
getting serious over the man, but she couldn't
resist taking him away from Mirabelle. Now he
wants to make it up with Mirabelle, and she
doesn't want to know—at least that's what she says,
but she's so miserable I'm sure she still loves him
...'

At this point she caught an amused glint in
Josie's eyes and sighed. 'I've gone off again, haven't
I?' she said sadly, and gave Josie an accusing look.
'You ought to have stopped me,' she said. 'Nat

always suggests a break for ten minutes while we get sorted out, back to the point we started at, I mean,' she grinned. 'Now where was I? Oh, yes, I was telling you about Jessica and Kade Boston, and the way she practically threw herself at him, and did she get a setdown! If it had been me I'd have crawled under the floorboards, but not her; it only spurred her on, and she's been trying ever since to get her hooks into him. Where he's concerned she's no pride—I guess it had to happen one day—they say the ones that have it all their own way eventually fall hard for someone who just doesn't want to know. I've no sympathy for her, she's hurt enough people in her time, so it's only right she sees the other side of it.'

The arrival of a customer cut short the rest of Lucy's confidences, and for the next half hour both the girls were busy, and as Lucy remarked with a wry grin when the last customer left and another one entered, 'We're either doing nothing, or over-worked—no happy in-between!'

Though the shop was a candy store, it also sold cigarettes and tobacco, and it was one of these items that the tall man in the stetson-type hat had come in to purchase. Josie, busy serving milk shakes to a group of young girls, became vaguely aware that she was under scrutiny from the other side of the store, and looked up to meet the cold grey eyes of a man she was sure she had seen somewhere before, yet where she had no idea, and it wasn't until she had served her last young customer that enlightenment came. Kade Boston! She was sure it was!

Josie looked over towards him again and saw

that he was now being served by Lucy. It was the short-sleeved silk shirt and tan slacks that he wore that had thrown her off the scent. The last time she had encountered him he had been dressed much as any other man that worked on a ranch would dress; now, in casual clothes, he presented an altogether different picture—apart from his eyes, she thought, and they were still as cold as before.

When he turned to leave the store, Lucy caught Josie's eye above the head of the small customer waiting to be served, and gave her a look that said plainly, 'Fancy that! and we were only just talking about him!'

The minute he left the store, Josie slipped the wisp of an apron from her waist and rushed to the door. 'I won't be a moment,' she told the surprised Lucy, and left before she could reply.

Her quarry was not far in front of her as she hurried after him. 'Mr Boston?' she called just before he was about to cross the street to a car parked on the other side of the road.

On hearing his name he stopped and turned round towards her, and stood waiting for her to join him. As she neared him, Josie sensed his impatience at being held up in this way, but she would never get this chance to speak to him again, and she was determined to talk to him.

'I won't keep you a minute,' she said breathlessly, and went on before she had had time to drew sufficient breath, so that her words seemed to tumble out rather than flow smoothly. 'It's about that fence,' she got out, noticing the haughty way his eyebrows rose at the subject. 'I wanted to tell you that I put it up, and not my grandfather.' At this point she ran out of steam, but her eyes were eloquent enough and matched his in coldness. There was a pause, and as he still did not reply she carried on, wishing she could wipe that supercilious look off his face. 'So I don't want my grandfather worried about it,' she added fiercely.

This he deigned to answer, and his views on the subject were shown in the grating, 'Your grandfather ...' he began, then whatever he was about to say he abruptly changed his mind about, as if it were of no consequence, and gave her a piercing look. 'I should have thought it would have been in your interests to leave things as they were,' he commented acidly. 'If I'd lost one animal through his neglect, I'd have had him out of that place pronto—I still can with a little co-operation,' he added meaningly.

Josie's eyes widened; what on earth did he mean? Her frown showed her puzzlement.

'Come now, Miss West,' he drawled, in what Josie could only interpret as an insulting tone, 'I'm sure that when you've thought about it, you'll get my meaning. Land these days is at a premium,' he shrugged disdainfully. 'I'm sure you could find somewhere for the pair of you to live, with plenty left over for the future.'

By now Josie had an inkling of what he was suggesting, but she had to be sure before giving him both barrels. 'What sort of co-operation had you in mind?' she asked sweetly.

His lips twisted at this, and Josie knew she had been right. Distaste was in every line of his face as he calmly looked her over. 'I should have thought a smart girl like you wouldn't need any prompting,' he drawled in the same insulting tone. 'However, I suggest you have a talk with him,' his lips thinned. 'You've seen the house and what state it's in. I wouldn't have thought it was all that comfortable to live in.' He gave her another hard stare. 'No doubt you've your reasons for living there,' he hinted sarcastically, 'but he might listen to you. I want that land, Miss West, and I'm willing to give a good price for it.' He paused for a moment, no doubt to give Josie time to dwell on this aspect, then said softly, 'There are such things as commissions, you know, and you could do very well out of it.'

Josie's hand itched to slap that haughty expression from his face, but she denied herself that pleasure for the moment anyway, and waited for him to go on, her eyes widening as she saw him put his hand in his top pocket and remove his wallet. He didn't intend to give her something on account, did he? she thought incredulously.

'My telephone number,' he announced grandly, as he selected a card from the wallet and handed it to her. 'If I'm not around, leave a message and I'll contact you later.'

Holding the card by the furthermost corner as if it were a poisonous insect, Josie let it flutter slowly to the ground without even affording it a glance, and saw with a pang of pleasure the way his eyes narrowed at the slight but definite snub she had just handed out to him. 'I don't think you could afford my commission, Mr Boston,' she said quietly. 'You'd be wise to forget about purchasing Carella; it's not for sale. As for "co-operating", as you put

it,' she added in a voice that matched his in coldness, 'you might like to know that it was I that
persuaded my grandfather not to sell up—not to
you, or anyone.'

'So you're hoping to up the price, are you?' he
ground out harshly, simply refusing to believe that
her actions couldn't be anything but mercenary.
'Well, I'm telling you now, and you can pass on
the message to that stubborn old man, that he'll
get the market price and no more. I've been more
than generous over the land I bought from him. I
might need that last acre, but I'm damned if I'm
having a gun pointed at my head—or haggle over
it. Have you any idea of what it cost me to replace
that fencing?' he demanded furiously.

Josie swallowed; now he would demand that
they should pay for it, and she couldn't see how—
not for a long time, as things were. 'We didn't ask
you to put it up,' she said defensively. 'I know
mine wasn't right for the job, but it would have
done until I could have afforded a better one.'

His thoughts were eloquent as he looked at her,
then back at the store. 'Earning that kind of
money?' he queried sarcastically.

Josie flushed; he did hit below the belt, didn't
he? 'It's just a fill-in,' she replied haughtily, 'until
I get a better job.'

'Schoolteaching?' he asked dryly. 'Well, it's my
guess you'll have a long wait. We've only one
school here, Miss West, as yet anyway, and if you're
relying on the new school needing staff, I might
remind you that certain recommendations will be
required—if you get my meaning,' he added suggestively.

Josie did get the message, and her blue eyes flashed as she answered bitingly, 'You've made your point, Mr Boston, now if you don't mind I ought to be getting back. I can't lose the only job I've been fortunate enough to get, can I?' and with her head held high, she swung away from him towards the store. Her feelings were mixed, she was furious, yet she could have wept with frustration. The wretched man had made her feel cheap and useless, and she didn't know which was worse. The only consolation was that he would not be likely to approach her grandfather now, and how she was going to pay him back for that fencing was beyond her comprehension, but one thing she did know was that she was not going to be beholden to him. She stopped in her tracks; she ought to have told him to let her have the bill and asked for time to pay.

Taking a deep breath, she turned and looked back, expecting to see him striding towards his car, but to her consternation he was still standing where she had left him. She flushed as she met his eyes, knowing that he must have seen her abrupt stop and now waited—for what? for her to change her mind? Well, he was going to be unlucky, she thought scathingly.

'Would you please let me have the bill for the fencing?' she requested quietly. 'It might take a while, but I'll do my best to clear it as soon as possible. If you've no objection to my paying by instalments, then that's how I'd have to do it.' Her eyes met his defiantly. He could insist on full payment then and there, she knew, but at least she had tried.

Josie was not sure whether his pause was deliberate or not, or whether he was genuinely considering her proposal, but when he spoke, it appeared he had given the matter some thought. 'If you really mean to pay your share, there is another way of doing it,' he said slowly.

A startled Josie stared at him. What other way could there be? Was he attempting to blackmail her into letting him get Carella? Then another thought struck her that made her cheeks flame a deep pink. There was no need for her to utter them, for they were mirrored in her eyes, and her colour deepened as she caught a look in Kade Boston's eyes that told her he knew what she was thinking.

'No, Miss West,' he said softly. 'It's neither of those possibilities. However, the idea is only just forming in my mind, and I'll have to work on it. I'll put it to you later, if I may?'

A stunned Josie could only nod her reply, and with a curt nod back at her, he left her to her musings and walked to his car.

Josie had still not recovered when she got back to the store, but on meeting Lucy's curious eyes, she made an attempt to pull herself out of her stupefied state by saying, 'Sorry about that, Lucy, but I just wanted a word with Mr Boston.'

Her hopes that Lucy would accept this bald statement without any comebacks were immediately dispelled as she saw Lucy give her a knowing grin. 'That's how he affects all the girls,' she said teasingly, then put her head on one side in a quizzing manner. 'Although somehow I couldn't see you chasing him!'

The remark was calculated to force Josie to tell her just what she had wanted to see Kade Boston about, and Josie, well aware of this, gave an exasperated sigh as she reluctantly rose to the bait. 'I was not chasing him,' she said dryly, and had to smile at Lucy's triumphant expression at the way her ruse had worked. 'I suppose you won't sleep tonight if I don't tell you what I wanted to see him about, will you?' she accused the now indignant Lucy; at least she tried to look indignant, but she didn't quite make it, for she was too anxious to hear what Josie had to tell her.

Josie replaced her apron before she continued, then wiped the counter down and noticing Lucy's worried look towards the door knew she was terrified someone would come in before she could hear the story, so she put her out of her misery. 'I was afraid he would ask Gramps to pay for the fencing,' she said quietly, and went on to tell her what had happened, and how Kade Boston had taken matters into his own hands and fenced the whole boundary.

When Josie had finished, Lucy's brow wrinkled in puzzlement. 'I don't see what you're worried about. If Kade Boston put that fence up, then he couldn't very well ask your grandfather to pay for it, could he?' she asked.

'Well, no,' conceded Josie hesitantly. 'I suppose he didn't think my efforts were good enough,' she finished lamely.

Lucy did not get the connection, and said so. 'But it doesn't matter now, surely? I mean, the fence is up, and as it was to protect his cattle— well, he foots the bill,' she argued reasonably.

Josie's blue eyes met Lucy's earnest brown ones. 'Oh, dear,' she sighed, 'I admit it does seem as if it ought to be simple, but it isn't. If you knew ...' She frowned; how could she make Lucy understand? 'Do you remember saying that Kade Boston reminded you of my grandfather?' she asked her abruptly, and at Lucy's slow nod, she continued with, 'Well, can you see Gramps accepting charity?' she demanded.

Lucy's eyes opened a shade wider, and she nodded again. 'I'm beginning to get your point,' she said slowly.

Josie gave an impatient shake of the head. 'No,' she said wearily. 'That's not strictly true,' and she gave a deep sigh. 'To be honest. he did accept it.' She gave Lucy a wry look. 'Saw things the way you saw them, that as he'd taken matters into his own hands, then he pays.'

'Well then,' Lucy broke in calmly, 'why are you worried? I don't get it—unless,' her eyes twinkled teasingly, 'you wanted a chance to tangle with our good-looking bachelor!'

'For goodness' sake!' exploded Josie. 'I'm not a bit interested in the man. and I certainly did not enjoy "tangling" with him, as you put it. I just had to make certain that he wouldn't send Gramps a bill. It wouldn't have mattered, you see, if I hadn't tried to cover that gap myself. I went to endless trouble to make sure that Grandfather knew nothing about it. Can't you see,' she asked the now sober Lucy, 'how he'd take the news that Kade Boston threw my efforts away as so much rubbish? Which he did—even though it was rubbish compared to the kind of barrier he put up. But that wouldn't matter to Gramps,' she said sadly. 'He'd be absolutely furious about it, and the fat would be in the fire.'

She was silent for a moment or so, then she added quietly, 'Gramps is an old man now—although he'd hate to hear me say so, and he's not as well as he ought to be. To be honest, I'm a bit worried about him ...' She faltered for a second, then said slowly, 'I had to prevent a clash between them. As you said earlier, Kade Boston doesn't mince his words, and I shudder when I think of what he might have said about my puny efforts at fencing that gap.'

Lucy hurried over to her side and squeezed her arm. 'Oh, Josie! I'm sorry I teased you, pet. I see now why you had to see him. Will it be all right now?' she asked anxiously.

Josie's gaze left the well-scrubbed wooden floor that she had been studying with a troubled look, and she met Lucy's kind eyes. 'I think so,' she said, but there was doubt in her voice. What, after all, had she really accomplished? Apart from telling him that it was she who was responsible for that apology for a fence, and not her grandfather. A frown creased her forehead; he was an intelligent man, and must have known why she had made a point of telling him this. As for the job he had hinted she might do—and it must be a job, she told herself—she hadn't a clue.

Lucy gave her arm another squeeze as if to remind her that she was still with her, for she had wandered off into a kind of reverie, and Josie came back to the present. Lucy had asked a question and she hadn't really answered it. 'As far as I can see,' she added a little belatedly. 'But I was right in thinking he did expect us to defray the cost of the fencing.'

'Oh, dear,' replied Lucy, drawing in her breath as if surprised. 'It doesn't sound a bit like Kade Boston to quibble over money. I suppose it's because he'd asked your grandfather to do it—and he hadn't—well,' she grimaced at Josie, 'not properly anyway, but he won't dun you, Josie. He's not like that—you'll see,' she said comfortably.

There were, Josie thought caustically, various ways of 'dunning', as Lucy had put it, but she did not say so, and for the rest of that morning both girls were kept busy and had no opportunity for further conversation, for which Josie was grateful. She had a lot on her mind and needed time to think about Kade Boston's extraordinary offer. She knew she ought to have told Lucy about it, but was afraid she might put a different interpretation on the whole thing—as indeed she herself had done—so she couldn't very well blame Lucy for thinking the same, and was able to stifle her conscience with the thought that nothing might come of whatever he had in mind.

At this thought Josie found herself shaking her head. She didn't know much about Kade Boston, and what she did know had come from either Nat or Lucy—but of one thing she was sure, and that was that he was not a man to make idle suggestions, and far from letting the matter drop. she was certain she would soon find herself wondering how she could cope with two jobs!

However hard Josie tried to stop herself dwelling on the subject, she constantly failed, and had

now got to the stage of wondering how her grandfather would take to the idea of her being forced to
work to pay off the debt they owed Kade Boston,
and her heart quailed at the thought of his reaction—in all probability he would order her to
have nothing to do with the man, and Josie would
be back to square one with a vengeance! The clash
she had hoped to avoid would then be a certainty.

Oh, why hadn't she let things be? Why hadn't
the man accepted the fact that they couldn't pay
and left it at that? He didn't need the money, did
he? Josie then miserably reminded herself that he
would probably have done just that if she hadn't
been foolish enough to offer to pay—even though
it be by instalments. Her pride of course had
forced her to make the offer, which, she told herself crossly, she wouldn't have done if he hadn't
brought the matter up.

By the time Josie got home that evening, she felt
as if she had been put through a wringer. Somehow she had to warn her grandfather of what
might be in store, but she was too weary to work
out the right approach to the subject, for it had to
be right. She had made an absolute mess of things
so far and couldn't risk making things worse. All
she could do now was to play a waiting hand, and
deal with the matter as and when necessary. There
was still a slim chance that she was meeting her
fences before she came to them, she reminded herself hopefully.

CHAPTER FIVE

HAPPILY for Josie, Dan Muntrose was calling on her grandfather later that evening to give him a game of chess, a pastime they used to indulge in before Joseph cut himself off from society, and this meant that he would rest directly after their evening meal, in order to be fresh for the coming skirmish on the chessboard. For Josie, it meant an evening's freedom in which to follow her own devices.

Although she had plenty to do to keep herself occupied, it wasn't long before she was thinking out ways and means of extricating herself from her earlier agreement with Kade Boston—not, she reminded herself sharply, that she had actually said anything, just nodded a little bewilderedly at him and he had assumed the rest! Her lips straightened as she stacked away the dishes she had just washed up. Now that she had had time to think things over, she didn't know what she was worrying about! She couldn't possibly do two jobs, and that was an end to the matter. He would just have to accept her first offer to pay by instalments—it was that or nothing, she thought darkly. She would write to him and make it quite clear that anything else was out of the question, for she already had a job—as she had reminded him after that snide remark of his on the slim chances of her obtaining a teaching post.

Her small chin jutted out as she recalled his attitude; he couldn't make her take another job, and she was certainly not going to let Nat and Lucy down. There was Billy too to be considered, and she had promised to help him.

Josie felt infinitely better now that her mind was made up, and not wanting to put off writing the letter for a moment longer, she went through to the sitting-rooom in search of writing materials.

The sound of voices coming from the back porch arrested her movement for a moment, then she remembered Dan, and relaxed. He was early, she thought, and she hoped her grandfather had had enough rest. However, a second later she froze in her tracks. That was definitely not Dan Muntrose's voice! And as her sensitive ears caught the slow lazy drawl of Kade Boston, her eyes widened. Oh, he wouldn't mention that fence, would he? If he so much as hinted ... Josie made for the back porch with the light of battle in her eyes.

The sight that met her eyes of the two men, by all accounts having an amiable discussion, nearly took her breath away, and although she breathed an inward sigh of relief, her eyes still remained stormy as she took in the way Kade Boston sat in the cane chair next to her grandfather's chair with his long legs splayed out in front of him in a completely relaxed manner, and the stormy look was replaced by a surprised but wary look, as she saw him get to his feet on her appearance.

The action completely threw Josie off her high horse, for she had come prepared to do battle with him for daring to worry her grandfather when she had particularly requested him not to do so.

Joseph West looked back at her still standing there, and her heart lifted when she saw him grin at her. 'Seems you're in demand,' he said gruffly with a hint of pride in his voice. 'Kade heard you were a teacher, and he's got a job for you. Said it wouldn't take long, didn't I? Thought you wouldn't be wasting your time in that shop for long,' he went on happily.

Mercifully for Josie the sound of a car coming up the front drive announced the arrival of Dan, and her grandfather got up. 'Well, I guess I'll leave you to work out the details,' he said cheerfully. 'My sparring partner's arrived,' and giving Kade an approving nod, and Josie a conspiratorial look, he went to greet his visitor.

Josie's astounded blue eyes met the enigmatical grey ones of Kade Boston. She didn't know how he had done it, but it looked as if it was all over bar the shouting, and she was about to do the shouting! 'I was going to write to you and tell you I couldn't possibly take on another job,' she said crisply, and watched his eyes narrow at the sudden attack.

He did not reply to this, but pointed a long imperious finger at the chair her grandfather had just vacated. 'Shall we talk it over?' he suggested mildly, yet Josie had a feeling that he was not going to take no for an answer, despite his casual manner.

Drawing a deep breath and with a nonchalance she was far from feeling, she sat down opposite him. 'How did you know I was a teacher anyway?' she demanded curiously, determined not to be

brow-beaten by this man who seemed to expect
people to jump to his bidding.

The question brought a smile to his lips and
relaxed the cold, haughty look of his, and Josie felt
a queer jerk somewhere in the region of her heart.
'Miss Plumstead,' he replied casually. 'She's the
local teacher,' he explained. 'You're coaching
young Billy Muntrose, aren't you? Well, it seems
he's come on well since you took him in hand, so
she made a few enquiries.'

Josie's stiff aggressive manner visibly relaxed at
this. He needn't have said that, need he? she
thought, and a feeling of accomplishment washed
over her at the thought that she had helped Billy
—and would go on helping him, she told herself
firmly, in spite of this man who seemed so determined to get his own way. She couldn't go on helping Billy if she had another job, could she?

Before she could say what was on her mind,
Kade drawled, 'I've a bit of a problem, you see. My
brother and his wife are in the wilds of Borneo at
the present time, and likely to be there for another
three months or so. They're botanists, by the way,
and as such, their work takes them all over the
world at any given time.' He drew in a deep
breath, as if impatient to explain the situation and
be done with it. 'As Borneo is not an ideal place to
take a child, I agreed to keep their daughter Maryanne with me until their return.' He took another
deep breath and gently flexed his strong fingers as
they lay along the side of the chair. 'I'm afraid
she's been a little spoilt in the past,' he told Josie
quietly. 'Usually she travels with her parents, and
has private tuition wherever they happen to be,

but this was one trip they couldn't take her on.'

Josie met his grey eyes warily. If he wanted her to coach this child as she was coaching Billy, then perhaps she could manage ... 'I tried sending her to the local school,' he went on slowly, 'but it didn't work out, and there was nothing for it but to remove her, for the good of the school, not to mention Miss Plumstead's peace of mind!' he added dryly, then shot Josie an interrogating look. 'I want you to take over the child's education while she's at Blue Mount.'

Josie drew in a tiny sigh of relief; if that was all it entailed, she could do it. The hours, of course, would have to be worked out. Nat wasn't so busy in the mornings, and if she gave the child an hour each morning, say from nine to ten, she could then go on to work ... She looked back at Kade to find him studying her with as much curiosity as she had previously studied him. 'Very well,' she said brightly. 'Might I suggest that I give her an hour each morning? From nine to ten would suit me perfectly.'

He frowned at this. 'I was thinking more on the lines of ten to four,' he answered slowly yet firmly.

Josie blinked in astonishment. Why, that was full time! Of all the nerve! Her lips closed tightly before she answered, 'Out of the question, I'm afraid,' with just as much firmness as he had shown, and the spark in her eyes bore out her feelings on the matter to prove that she meant what she said, then she stood up quickly to indicate that the interview was over, on her part anyway!

Kade Boston did not move, but sat there watching her with a speculative look in his eyes, and this irritated Josie beyond measure, for she knew he was summing her up, then still without a word he pointed to the chair again. But Josie stood her ground. 'Nine to ten, Mr. Boston. I'm afraid that's all the time I can give; if you can't accept that, then that's all there is to say.' She gave him a level look. 'We do have to eat, you know,' she added meaningly, just in case he had overlooked this fact, but wealthy as he was, she doubted if this point had occurred to him.

His expressive brows shot up at this last remark of hers, but that long forefinger of his still pointed at the chair. 'Sit down, Miss West,' he said softly. 'We haven't finished yet.'

'I have,' retorted Josie furiously, thinking how intent he was on getting his pound of flesh.

'But I haven't,' he replied in a soft but deadly voice that warned her to watch her words. 'Now calm down and listen to my proposition. I'm fully aware that you have to earn a living—well—you will—and you won't find me ungenerous. If you take the job I shall consider the debt paid. All you earn will be yours, to do whatever you wish with; I can't say fairer than that, can I?' he drawled dryly.

Josie's eyes widened. Forget the debt? But that was the only reason she had agreed, if only tacitly, to the arrangement. Her soft mouth set in a stubborn line as she replied in a voice that held a hint of pride in it, 'You're very kind, but I'm afraid it's still out of the question. Nat and Lucy Muntrose have also been very kind to me, and I have no intention of letting them down, and as you mentioned earlier, there's Billy to consider, too. He still needs extra coaching, so you see, under the circumstances ...' She was silent for a second or so, then glancing up at him she flushed as she took note of the way his gaze slowly travelled over her slight figure and came back to her now indignant eyes, for she had caught a trace of amusement in his as if the very idea of her opposing him was causing him some entertainment. 'As for forgetting the debt,' she ground out, 'I couldn't possibly agree to that—it was,' she added in a bitter-sweet voice calculated to take that amused look out of his eyes, 'the only reason I could even contemplate your proposition.'

Kade hadn't liked that one bit, she thought with a flash of triumph as she saw the amused look replaced by one of fury, then his heavy lids were lowered to mask his feelings.

Although he must have been seething, his voice was as controlled as it had been before as he drawled matter-of-factly, 'You do appear to have misjudged me, Miss West. I did not forget Billy, and I've made arrangements for him to attend the classes at Blue Mount.' He gave Josie full time to digest this, and then continued in a haughty voice, 'It will be a small class, you understand—my niece, Billy Muntrose, and three other children who are in dire need of education. The three other children are also staying at Blue Mount—er—their fathers are in my employment.' The ice in his eyes was echoed in his voice as he continued coldly, 'As for letting Nat and Lucy down, they'll have no difficulty in filling the vacancy, I can assure you. I've had a word with them on this, and they're quite willing to release you.'

Josie was stunned, and her wide blue eyes registered the shock he had given her, making that amused look return to his eyes as he watched her reaction.

The stunned look was soon replaced by one of fury. How dared he? Without so much as a 'do you mind?' he had adjusted affairs to suit his purpose, making Josie feel like a puppet on a string—made to move only when directed by the man manipulating the strings—Kade Boston! As for Nat and Lucy, of course they would have agreed, she thought mistily; they would have considered it a good opportunity for her and wouldn't have dreamed of standing in her way—but did Nat really want Billy taken away from the local school? He had not been in favour of it before when Lucy had hinted at Josie taking over his entire education.

She drew a deep breath, and her fuming eyes met the now mocking ones of the man who sat watching her so calmly. 'If you don't mind, I'd prefer to have a word with Nat on this before committing myself,' she said stiffly, adding on a note of fury, 'Do you always expect people to jump to your bidding, just like that? As if they had no will of their own?' she demanded furiously.

The mocking light was still in his eyes as he replied softly, 'Only when necessary, Miss West, and I think,' he added in a soft maddening drawl, 'that you'll eventually see that in this case the arrangement is eminently suitable all round.' He gave an offhand shrug of his powerful shoulders. 'If it's the matter of the debt that's worrying you, then I shall deduct a small amount each month until it's cleared.' He stood up abruptly, and gave

Josie a hard searching look. 'Now, have you any other objection? I take it you do want to do the work you were trained for?' he asked bluntly.

Josie's indignant eyes met his cold ones, and she was forced to answer crossly, 'Of course I do!' There was much more she would have liked to add to this, but he gave her no chance of a comeback by giving a curt nod as if satisfied on this point at least. 'Then I shall expect you at ten on Monday. Use the main entrance, will you? Nat will show you the way,' he ordered brusquely, and placing his stetson on his head and giving the completely bemused Josie another curt nod, he took his leave of her.

For a few seconds Josie stood right where she was, as if she had taken over the role of puppet, and now that her master had left would remain lifeless until his return. Then she gave herself a mental shake; she must be going soft in the head. The trouble was, she had never met anyone like Kade Boston before, although she doubted that two such men could exist. She frowned; Lucy had said he reminded her of her grandfather when he was younger, and she slowly shook her head. Her grandfather wouldn't have trampled on people the way Kade Boston was trampling on her, and not only on her, but on Nat and Lucy too, unless she was very much mistaken.

On this thought she marched into the hall and to the telephone. She would speak to Nat then and there; Mr High and Mighty Boston might think it was all cut and dried, but it wasn't—not until she had ascertained Nat's feelings on the matter.

Her fingers started to dial the number; Nat

wouldn't hold out on her. He would tell her what he really thought about it. Her dialling finger poised on the last number as a thought suddenly struck her—but would he? He certainly wouldn't if he thought he would be standing in her way by refusing to accommodate Kade Boston, and Josie was sure Kade Boston would have rammed that point home to ensure Nat's co-operation. So just asking Nat for his thoughts on the matter would produce only confirmation.

Josie replaced the receiver slowly. This wasn't the way to do it. She had to go and see Nat and Lucy. She knew Nat well enough to be able to judge his real feelings on the matter, Lucy too, by now, and neither of them could fool her into believing they were satisfied with the arrangement if they thought otherwise.

With her grandfather busy with his game of chess with Dan, Josie wouldn't have a better opportunity to straighten things out before her grandfather became aware of the situation, for she was in no doubt of the advice he would give her on the matter, and it certainly wouldn't be in Nat and Lucy's favour—not because he preferred Kade Boston to Nat—but because he wanted Josie to take her rightful place in the profession she had trained for.

Collecting a light cardigan, for the evenings were a little on the cool side, Josie sneaked a quick look in to the sitting-room and found that as she had thought, Dan and her grandfather were completely engrossed in a world of their own, and all attention was focused on the board in front of them. Although Josie did give a casual, 'Won't be long, Gramps,' she was sure neither players heard her, and she smiled as she slipped out of the house.

On the way to the store, she thought about Kade Boston and how by rights she ought to have welcomed the chance to do the work she was trained for, and if it hadn't been for the autocratic way he had handled the situation, she would probably have jumped at the opportunity. As it was, she found herself actually hoping to find Nat and Lucy in full agreement with her own thoughts on the matter, and regretting their earlier decision—if it had been their decision, she thought scathingly, for when a man like Kade Boston wanted something he would leave no stone unturned to achieve his aim. He had as good as agreed with her on this point—no half measures with Mr Kade Boston!

By the time Josie had reached the store, she had convinced herself that aided and abetted by Nat and Lucy, she would make Kade Boston look elsewhere for someone to teach his niece! There was still the debt to be repaid, though, she mused thoughtfully, and once again she wished she had not been so conscientious as to offer to pay their share, and if he had been as fine a gentleman as everybody seemed to think he was, he wouldn't have taken her up on the offer. It wasn't as if he were a poor man and needed the money, she told herself darkly, but what he did need was someone to teach an obviously obnoxious child, and had seen a way of making use of Josie. As she jabbed the bell outside the side door of the store that led to Nat's private quarters, her finger pressed harder on the button when she recalled the calm way he had told her that Nat would show her the way to

Blue Mount—as if Nat were an employee of his!

Ten minutes later, however, Josie found the only one who was being aided and abetted was Kade Boston! And she was the only one taking a stand against him!

'Honestly, Josie, it's a chance for you to do the work you want to do,' urged an earnest Lucy. 'And we don't mind Billy attending classes at Blue Mount one bit—in fact, we're rather proud that Kade made a point of including him—aren't we, Nat?' she appealed to her husband.

Josie's hopes that Nat might not see things quite the same way as Lucy were completely dashed as she saw his confirming nod accompanied by the familiar grin. 'Sure am,' he answered. 'Thing is, we'll have a job in cutting young Billy down to size afterwards. He's already kidding himself he's as good as on the payroll of the biggest cattle ranch in Texas!'

On seeing that Josie was still not entirely convinced, for she was eyeing the pair of them with what could only be described as a suspicious look, if not an accusing one, Lucy carried on in the same theme, saying how marvellous it would be for Josie getting such an opportunity so early after her return home.

Josie wished she could wholeheartedly agree with her, but she had a curious sensation of letdown, and felt that everybody was ganging up on her. She wanted to teach, of course, but she would have liked the chance of choosing not only where she would teach, but who would employ her—and she indignantly muttered as much.

To her extreme annoyance, instead of gaining

his sympathy, Nat gave her a wide grin. 'Well,' he drawled in that characteristic way of his, 'you haven't been unhappy so far, have you?'

'Of course I haven't!' Josie retorted quickly, not really seeing what Nat was getting at.

'Well then,' went on Nat carefully, 'same boss, but different job. You'll be okay, Josie.'

Josie stared at him. What did he mean by the same boss? She worked for Nat, didn't she?—or did she? Her eyes widened as the implication hit her—Kade Boston didn't own the store, did he? Oh no! She swallowed quickly. 'Are you telling me that Kade Boston owns the store?' she demanded accusingly to Nat.

Nat's eyes met Lucy's briefly before he answered, as if seeking her approval for what he was about to tell Josie, and on receiving an answering nod from her, he gave a wry smile. 'On paper, yes,' he began slowly. 'You'll remember me telling you that there were a lot of debts outstanding when I took over the store,' he gave a slight shrug. 'To be honest, I couldn't see myself clearing them in time to give us a decent living, and was seriously considering selling up.' His glance centred again on his wife, and softened as he continued, 'Well, Lucy didn't want that. The place was home to her, she was born here, remember. So we tried to find some other way of settling the debts and hanging on until it started to pay for itself.'

He paused for a second and searched for his cigarettes, then lit one, and after inhaling deeply, carried on, 'My dad had a pretty good idea of how things were, although we tried not to worry him with our problems, but before we knew it, he'd cooked up this scheme of selling up his place and going into lodgings. He knew there wasn't room for him here—we had three kids then. He'd got it all worked out that the cash he got from the house would have settled the more pressing debts, which it would have done, but we didn't want that for obvious reasons. There was no guarantee that the place would pay for itself, and we'd have felt pretty bad about things if we failed.' He took another pull on his cigarette. 'Things were pretty dicey for a while; I was trying to stall Dad from selling up, and looking for a job elsewhere to keep the wolf from the door.'

He looked up from studying his cigarette and met Josie's startled eyes. 'We still don't know the ins and outs of it, we can only guess that Kade somehow found out how things were, probably from Dad, although how we can't imagine. Dad's not one to blab about our affairs, or anyone's affairs come to that. The next thing we knew Kade offered to help us out by loaning us the necessary cash—without,' he said slowly and deliberately, 'any strings attached—and I mean that, Josie. I pay what I can, when I can, and that was two years ago. It's going to be a little while yet before I can wipe the slate clean, but mark this—not once in all this time has he referred to that debt. He acknowledges the payments, of course, by letter only—and apart from us, and Dad, who had to know—and now you—not a single soul knows of the transaction.'

He gave Josie a long appraisal before he added gravely, 'So you see, Josie, we've a good reason to respect Kade. We're mighty grateful to him, too. He's a fine man, as you'll find out in time.'

Josie's glance left Nat and rested on the carpeted floor. She was at a loss to know what to say, and could hardly back out of the arrangement now, not after a disclosure like that. Besides, it was obvious that Lucy and Nat wanted her to oblige Kade Boston. She sighed inwardly as she looked away from the red and grey patterned carpet, and said quietly, 'He said you would show me the way to the front entrance on Monday.'

That was all she said, and both Nat and Lucy let out a breath of pure relief, and the relief echoed in Nat's voice as he answered swiftly, 'Sure thing. Er ... Lucy tells me you drive?' He looked quickly at Josie, and at her confirming nod, grinned, 'Well, there's an old Ford in the garage. It needs a bit of attention, but I can get it fixed by Monday—used to belong to a cousin of Lucy's who sorta forgot to collect it after he took off for high school last autumn, and we kinda thought you might get some use out of it. I'd be mighty grateful if you'd take it,' he added earnestly. 'I need all the space I can get now that business is looking up, and that machine's been there a sight too long. Don't worry about Harry suddenly claiming it—he told me to get rid of it—he's taken to much smarter jobs these days!' he chuckled.

Although Josie was grateful for the offer, and accepted smilingly, she couldn't rid herself of the same odd sensation she had experienced soon after Kade Boston had left her a short while before— that of being a puppet and having another's will thrust upon her, and even though the conversation changed to other subjects for the remainder of her visit, she couldn't throw off the feeling of helplessness, for she had a strong premonition that her entire future would be somehow linked with the man who was now holding the strings, and it was not a comforting feeling. She had been master of her ship for too long to stand aside and just let anyone take over the controls. It meant a few squalls ahead, and Josie was all for a peaceful existence, but not at the cost of her independence!

On her way back home, she found herself marvelling at the sudden change of manner shown by Kade Boston, not only to her, but to her grandfather too. He had been almost polite; and that meant she had to be on her guard, for she was sure he still nursed hopes of obtaining Carella. She paused in her stride. Was that why he had offered her the job? Oh, he needed someone to teach his niece, all right—but surely he could have got someone else? The salary he could afford to offer would have assured that. She wriggled a small stone out of her sandal, before she started off again. She had been so mad at the way Kade had handled things, she hadn't given his earlier words much thought—of course he still wanted Carella, enough to take someone he considered a gold-digger on his payroll, and she had so very nearly been hoodwinked into thinking he had chosen her because of her prowess with Billy.

And what, she thought shrewdly, was she supposed to do when the job folded up? There would not be another vacancy at the store. She couldn't expect Nat and Lucy to take her on again. The answer was not long in coming; she wouldn't need a job! Not if Kade Boston succeeded in getting Carella—he'd hinted at a respectable remuneration for her in getting her co-operation, hadn't he?

Josie gave a sigh of pure exasperation—was she slow! Her chin jutted out in defiance. Well, she had got there at last! She didn't know what tactics were going to be used on her, or her grandfather, come to that, but if she kept her head, and her distance, she ought to be able to stay at least one step ahead of whatever machinations Kade Boston had in mind to obtain his goal!

CHAPTER SIX

THE following Monday morning, Nat called for Josie in good time to get her to Blue Mount by ten o'clock, driving a pale blue Ford, that in Josie's eyes certainly could not be called in the least dilapidated, but she knew most Americans rarely kept any model for much over a year.

While she listened to the happy banter between her grandfather and Nat, she tried to quell her fluttering nerves at the thought of what lay ahead, for she had gone through several stages of rehearsal as to what manner she would adopt on her next meeting with Kade Boston. It wouldn't do, she told herself, to let him know she was fully aware of the reason why she had been offered the job. As for the niece—if she were half as spoilt as Kade Boston had intimated, then perhaps there might be a way of turning things to her advantage. For instance, if the child gave her any trouble, or insolence, then all she need do was walk out on the job—even Kade Boston couldn't blame her for that, and she would have tried, wouldn't she?

The more Josie dwelt on this distinct possibility, the more cheerful she became. Her grandfather would heartily endorse such an action, for he was a great stickler for convention, and had often read the young Josie a lecture on the lines of manners making man, and costing nothing, and the rebellious Josie would be made to apologise to whoever it was that she had offended. Josie hadn't thought at that time that the training would have stood her in good stead in the years that followed, but it had, and could now prove to be the solution to the dilemma she was now in.

On the way to Blue Mount, Nat's cheerful chatter eased the apprehension that in spite of her previous musings still hovered around her, and the fact that he had elected that she should drive the car to get used to the controls also took her mind off her troubles, giving her something else to concentrate on. After the first mile Josie was completely in control. The Ford differed from its English counterparts, for it was automatic, and a delighted Josie soon found time to take in the scenery as well as keeping the car on a straight track.

They were just entering the boundaries of the ranch when it suddenly struck her that Billy should have been with them, and she asked Nat why he wasn't.

'Picked up some tummy bug,' answered Nat. 'Guess he'll be okay in a day or so, but we didn't want to risk any of the other kids picking it up. Doc says there's a lot of whatever it is around. It's not serious, just one of these things kids get occasionally. He's mighty put out at missing the first day, I can tell you,' he grinned, then as he looked ahead he said, 'The next turning on the left, Josie, then straight on. You'll see the ranch-house long before we come to it. We follow the drive-in and bear to the right of the house—the garages are at the back of the house.'

When they eventually arrived at the main entrance to Blue Mount, Josie could well appreciate why Nat had felt a car would come in useful—not only useful, but absolutely essential, she thought with a wry grimace. It was all of six miles from Carella, if not more, and however Kade Boston had expected her to get there without transport, she couldn't think. A nasty suspicion then struck her that perhaps it had been he who had suggested the use of a car for her to Nat. It must be common knowledge that her grandfather did not own a car. Even in the days of the market garden, he had never bothered to purchase one. All products that had to be transported any distance were collected by a trucking firm, or taken in Dan Muntrose's small van to the nearby town.

Josie blinked quickly in an effort to dispel these unwelcome thoughts. It was just the sort of thing Nat and Lucy would do, and why she had to credit Kade Boston with every single happening was beyond her, although, a tiny voice whispered unrepentantly inside her, it would also be just the thing he would think of too. He would not be likely to overlook such a detail, not when it concerned the making or breaking of his project!

As Nat had said, the ranch-house was in full view even at this distance, and Josie's curious eyes took in the house and the surrounding grounds. No wonder he thought Carella was on its last legs, she thought, for she doubted whether a greater comparison could be found than that between her grandfather's house, and the architectural dwelling in front of her. The roof tiles of the house she was staring at had a blue grey tint that shimmered in the light of the morning, yet had a cool look about them. There had been no additions made here, she mused, to the original structure, not that she had ever been to the ranch before, for the previous owner had been a bachelor, she recalled, and a very unsociable one at that, but she had heard gossip about the run-down state of the property when she was a child, and how the more daring children would make the ramshackle outbuildings their play centres, always keeping a wary eye out for the short-tempered owner of the property.

It appeared that not only the previous dwelling place had been demolished, but the grounds too had undergone drastic change, she thought as she guided the car past the immaculately kept lawned areas and flower gardens that surrounded the house, and followed the bend to the right as indicated by Nat, into a courtyard at the back of the house, and drew up by the side of a four-car garage, and what most probably was the stabling area, for there were several outbuildings lying slightly further back from the garage.

After congratulating her on a smooth run, Nat led the way past the garage to a finely wrought ornamental gate set in a side wall attached to the garage, and down a short bush-scented avenue towards a low-slung white-painted building, and Josie, following his bright checked shirt, was a little amazed that he should know his way so well—either that, or he had been given precise instructions as to where to take her. Either way, it didn't help to squash the butterfly feeling in her stomach as her apprehension grew as they neared the door of the building they were approaching, and she hardly heard Nat's enthusiastic meanderings on the way Kade had improved the property. There was, however, one little consolation for Josie, and that was that if this was the schoolroom then it was far enough way from the ranch-house to ensure a certain amount of privacy. It also meant that she would not be liable to run into Kade Boston each day, and for this she was extremely grateful.

The door was open, and though she knew they were expected, the sight of that open door made her feel like a fly about to walk into a web, and hardly helped calm her nerves.

Meeting the cool grey eyes of Kade Boston the minute they stepped inside the door of the building, and realising her earlier hopes had been slightly misplaced, added to her misery, and her lovely blue eyes echoed her feelings more than she knew.

'Good morning, Miss West,' Kade drawled, yet his eyes showed his pleasure at her appearance, as if, she thought perplexedly, that he hadn't been too sure she would come. 'Thanks a lot, Nat,' he nodded to Josie's companion. 'Borrow the station waggon, I'll get someone to collect it later.'

Nat murmured his thanks, and giving the reluctant Josie a little push further into the room, said teasingly, 'Over to you, teacher!' and made his departure.

A small child detached herself from a desk further down the room and came to stand next to Kade, her hand creeping up to grasp his large brown one, while her wide brown eyes openly studied Josie.

'This is Maryanne,' Kade introduced, and

looked down at the child beside him. 'Maryanne, this is Miss West, the lady I told you about, and mind you do what you're told. I shall be extremely displeased if I hear that you've not behaved yourself,' he admonished lightly as he gave the child's thick brown curls a light ruffle.

The child did not answer, but continued to study Josie, then looked up at her uncle. 'Are you going to stay and see if everything's all right?' she asked in a thin reedy autocratic voice that Josie immediately took exception to, as well as the suggested implication that Josie might not be suitable for the job!

Kade frowned, and glanced at Josie, giving her a sympathetic grin, then released his hand from Maryanne. 'Certainly not!' he said in a no-nonsense voice. 'I've more to do than watch over your scholarly progress. Did you bring the folder I asked you to bring with you?' he asked the now mutinous child.

Maryanne gave a little shrug of her dainty shoulders and turned towards the desk she had been sitting at; one that was in direct line with the teacher's desk, Josie noticed, as her depressed gaze followed the slight figure as she went to collect the folder her uncle had spoken of. No ordinary jeans for this child, Josie thought, but a pair of beautifully tailored denims cut in pinafore style and matching blue and white blouse.

Josie's gaze left the child and rested on the man standing beside her, and as she caught a glint of amusement in his eyes, her lips folded in a straight line. He *would* think it was funny! It looked as if the child was going to be every bit as tiresome as she had thought she would be. She turned her attention elsewhere and looked about the room. Whatever the place had been used for before, it certainly made an ideal makeshift school. There was even an old blackboard, Josie noted, and with the five desks in position, it really did look as if she had begun her career at last—or would, if there were any other pupils to teach. She knew about Billy, but what of the others?

Accurately interpreting her thoughts, Kade said as he glanced at his watch, 'They'll be here in precisely ten minutes,' and taking the folder from Maryanne, he added, 'I wanted a word with you before you start. Shall we go outside?' and without waiting for Josie's answer he walked ahead of her and out of the building.

A reluctant Josie followed his broad back, and wondered if he was going to tell her what salary he would be paying her, and what amount he would deduct each month to pay off the debt. She was almost certain that this was his intention, for when he saw that Maryanne had followed her out of the building and now stood a little way behind Josie, he said quietly but authoritatively, 'Wait inside, will you, Maryanne?'

A petulant expression showed that Maryanne did not like this one little bit, but she knew her uncle well enough to obey the instruction without complaint, and with a toss of the head she ran back into the schoolroom, slamming the door behind her.

With her eyes on the shut door, Josie asked curiously, 'How old is Maryanne?'

Kade gave her a wicked grin before he replied,

'Ten, I'm afraid. I guess she acts more adult than she really is. She hasn't had much to do with children of her own age. I'm hoping to make her parents see sense over this. Do her the world of good to learn to give and take a little. As I told you previously, she's used to travelling around with her parents and getting a sight more attention than is good for her.' His eyes met Josie's. 'Don't tell me she's a spoilt little madam—I know that. I'm just hoping you'll accept the challenge. It's not going to be easy, I know, but somehow I've an idea that she's met her match in you.'

His brows raised as he said this, as if inviting Josie's comments, but she remained silent, digesting only the fact that he had just calmly demolished her one and only hope for her early departure from the scene. In other words, she thought despondently, he would accuse her of cowardice if she threw the job up! Very clever of him. He must want Carella badly, she thought scathingly, even to the extent of pushing his niece into the fray!

Giving a little sigh at her continued silence, he went on to other matters, and it was not salary, or what he would deduct, but concerned the other children. 'I want you to keep an eye out for what they need,' he said, his voice reverting back to the authoritative tone. 'And I mean clothing as well as school equipment. No need to speak to the children; just mention it to me when you see me, and I'll do the rest. I think you'll find you've all you need in the stationery line. I've had a word with Miss Plumstead on the textbooks required, so you should find you've everything you want—if not, make a list out of your requirements and I'll see you have them.'

He hesitated as his eyes fell on three children walking up the narrow path towards the school. 'You'll find all of them are in need of schooling, and that goes for Maryanne too. As you'll see by this folder, she's a little behind the average level for her age. As for the others,' his eyes rested on the children as they neared them, 'their fathers can't read or write, they've never bothered, and the kids were quite willing to follow in their footsteps—now, that is—but give them a year or two and they'll wish otherwise. Oh, they've had a smattering of education, when they felt like turning up at school, that was, but the absent periods were getting more and more frequent.' He smiled at Josie, and she wished he wouldn't do that; his smiles had a way of breaking down her defences.

'It got to be a vicious circle; when they did attend, they'd find they were so far behind that it meant they were placed with the much younger children. As you know, there's only the one school —at the present time, anyway, and like Billy, they need closer supervision.' He gave her a rueful look. 'You've got your work cut out, I'm afraid, there's no budding Einsteins in this group. But I'd be very grateful if you'd have a go at bringing them in line with the average level for their ages so that they can attend the new school when it opens.'

Put that way, how could Josie turn it down? She couldn't, she had been made to feel very special, and although she tried not to dwell on this point too much. something glowed inside her and lit up a tiny light at the back of her eyes.

The children had been talking amongst themselves and had not noticed that they were observed, or that the boss of Blue Mount stood awaiting their arrival. When they became aware of their audience, they pulled up sharply and stood silent with awkward embarrassment in front of Josie and Kade.

'Well on time, I see,' remarked Kade as he gave them an approving nod, then he directed Josie's attention to the taller boy. 'This is Pedro, Miss West; he's the oldest by a year—and this,' he nodded at the boy standing next to Pedro, 'is Juan—you're ten, aren't you, Juan?'

The boy nodded, but said nothing, his black eyes warily darting from Kade to Josie, as he shuffled back a little in order to let the small boy standing a little way behind him take over the limelight and be introduced. 'And you're Miguel,' Kade commented dryly, duly noting the way the smaller boy had been made to take his share of the unwelcome attention.

'I think you'll find them attentive pupils, Miss West,' he commented, in the tone of voice that suggested they had better be attentive—or else!

A few minutes later Kade took his leave of them, remarking again to Josie that if there was anything she required she was to let him know, and a partially relieved Josie ushered the boys into the schoolroom to join Maryanne, who sat in isolated splendour at her desk.

It was obvious that the boys were acquainted with the fact that they would be sharing lessons with the boss's niece, for they barely glanced in her direction after their first quick look, and moved with reluctant steps towards the desks.

'You may sit there,' indicated a gracious Mary-anne to Pedro, pointing to the desk next to hers in a manner of conferring an honour on him, which was not at all appreciated by the scowling Pedro.

'I think we'll let Pedro choose his own desk,' intervened Josie smoothly. 'He'll probably want to sit next to Juan, anyway,' she added for good measure, not failing to note the quick flash of temper this calm but authoritative statement produced from Maryanne, and sighed inwardly. It was going to be uphill all the way, she thought, and this was only the beginning.

Pedro chose the desk farthest away from the one Maryanne had indicated, and to make matters worse, from Maryanne's point of view anyway, there was a mad scramble from the remaining two boys to secure the other desk in a similar position on the other side of her. Juan, being the biggest of the two, won the tussle, and Miguel had no choice but to accept what was left—either way, it meant sitting next to the girl, and darting the triumphant Juan an accusing look, Miguel settled himself next to Pedro, disclaiming any previous friendship with Juan.

'Right, then,' said Josie with more assurance than she felt as she walked to her desk and put the folder that contained Maryanne's prowess in the educational line down on the desk for future perusal. 'I think we'll spend the first morning find-ing out what standards you've reached in various subjects. Would you look in your desks and see if you have any exercise books there?' she asked. 'I shall want you to write down the answers to some questions I shall be giving you.'

'I put exercise books in all the desks,' piped up Maryanne importantly. 'And pens,' she added as an afterthought, looking from the boys to Josie as if she expected to be congratulated for such fore-sight.

'Thank you, Maryanne,' answered Josie drily, sure that Kade had been the instigator of this act, although she did not say so. Maryanne's aplomb needed a little balm right then after the extremely ungentlemanly actions of her classmates.

So the morning progressed, and Josie was soon in possession of her pupils' rather undistinguished scholastic attainments. While the children were laboriously writing out the answers to her ques-tions, she took the opportunity of studying Mary-anne's school report, and was relieved to see that she was at least two grades below the normal standard for her age. Had she been an exception-ally bright child, Josie would have had the added worry of her being held back by the rest of the class. As it was, Maryanne was just as much in need of extra coaching as were the boys. Kade, she mused, must have known this, and she had a shrewd idea that the local teacher had drawn his attention to the matter.

That week passed and then another, and Josie found herself thoroughly enjoying the challenge, for as Kade had said, it was a challenge. Ways had to be found to keep the children interested in the lessons, particularly as it was branding time on the ranch—so Josie learnt from Pedro, who obviously wished he were elsewhere, but contented himself with regaling tales of past round-ups to the avid Billy, who would listen with wide eyes, drinking in every word Pedro uttered. Juan and Miguel, although brought up on the same tales, for they were handed down from father to son and went back to the early settlers in those parts, listened with just as much reverence. Maryanne, too, although she tried hard to hide her interest, particularly as she had welcomed Billy as a knight in shining armour on his arrival to the class a few days after school had begun. His politeness and willingness to listen to anything she said had acted as a tranquilliser on her frustrated feelings, but alas, this happy state of affairs did not last long, for although Billy was still polite, his allegiance was soon transferred to Pedro.

It was an unfair competition that Maryanne lost hands down, and Josie came to dread the break periods when these tales were regaled, and tried to bring up subjects to discuss that would interest all her pupils, and in which all could take part—but she too lost hands down—for an innocent-sounding question from Billy to Pedro would invariably turn the conversation to ranch life, leaving Josie with a truculent Maryanne to deal with.

Lunch was served in an annexe adjoining the schoolroom, and Josie was thankful she had elected to go back to Carella. She had had a valid excuse for this, as she had wanted to check up on her grandfather, and get him a meal. As things turned out, she found she needed that hour's break away from the children, and would return refreshed and ready for the fray.

If Maryanne had only been allowed to have

lunch as she had presumed she would, with her uncle at Blue Mount, it would have meant an easing of the frustrations building up inside the child at the lack of attention she was receiving, from her point of view, from all and sundry. But Kade had meant what he had said about it being time she learnt to live with other children, and adamantly stuck to this policy by insisting that she stayed right through the day with her classmates, as she would have done had she been at any other school.

There were times when Josie was tempted to ask Kade to allow Maryanne this one concession, although she was well aware that he was perfectly right in his reasoning, and in view of this she resisted the temptation. For one thing, he might accuse her of backing out of the challenge, and for another, Josie wished to keep the relationship between herself and Kade on a business footing.

Her hopes that she might not see a great deal of him during school hours were gratified, but he made a point of seeing her once a week and would appear just before school finished on a Friday to have a word with her on the week's progress, also to find out if there was anything she required—or that the children required.

To his question of whether Maryanne had behaved herself, Josie would always give a cautious answer, only too well aware of the twinkle in his eyes that belied his straight face, and the way he continually watched her, even when he should have been looking at Maryanne's progress sheet that Josie prepared for him each week.

It did occur to her that perhaps he was looking

for signs of strain. He must have known—or indeed heard from Maryanne—of the squabbles that would break out now and again between the children, or to be more correct between Maryanne and the four boys, and how she, Maryanne, would be the one to be corrected, and nothing was said to the boys.

In this she would be perfectly correct, but as she was the one who had instigated the squabble by some mischiefmaking remark about some of the boys' work, it was only right that she should be the one reprimanded, as Josie had taken great pains to inform her at the time.

Whatever complaints Maryanne had voiced to him, Kade never repeated them to Josie, and she was forced to admit grudgingly to herself that even if he did have an ulterior motive in employing her, he was a just man.

This was not the only admission Josie had had to make during the first few weeks at Blue Mount. As time passed, she found it increasingly harder to place Kade in the role of a double-dealer. It didn't jell somehow, not with all Josie had learnt about him, not only from Nat and Lucy, but from the boys whose fathers were employed by him.

As their names suggested, and by their black hair and eyes, the boys came of Mexican stock. Their fathers were cattlemen, as were their fathers before them, and had, Josie gleaned, had a thin time of it for several years before Blue Mount started up in the locality. To have regular wages and a roof over their heads was something even the children could appreciate, and did.

At the end of each week Josie would find herself

looking forward to, yet dreading, the meeting with
Kade. His rare smiles were getting through to her,
and although she tried to remind herself that they
meant nothing personally to her, and that he was
just being pleasant, it didn't stop her pulse rate
rising, and she would reprimand herself for her
stupidity. Before she knew it she would be blush-
ing like a teenager. At this thought she went cold;
Kade Boston saw a little too much for her liking,
and she had a shrewd suspicion that he was not
unaware of the flutter of her pulse rate during
those end-week sessions.

Thoughts such as these helped Josie to keep on
an even keel. Kade was an experienced man, in
more ways than one, she told herself darkly, recalling what Lucy had said about him earlier. For
instance, the way he had put that girl in her place
when she had all but thrown herself at him. He
would, she mused, recognise such a gambit from
way off, and Josie was sure it wouldn't have been
the first occasion he had had to give such a set-
down; in all probability he was an old hand at the
game.

He might not, Josie told herself, realise just how
devastating those slow smiles of his were, and in
that case could hardly be blamed for the resultant
flutterings in the feminine breast. She shook her
head slowly. Kade Boston was not a man who did
things by accident—accidentally-on-purpose, yes—
that was more in his line of reasoning.

Having worked that much out, Josie had a
strange sensation in the pit of her stomach. Those
smiles had been getting pretty frequent lately, and

took her back to her first suspicions as to why she had been offered the job. She had to be on his side if he wanted Carella, didn't she? Was this the softening-up process? she wondered; if so, half the battle was won, if he did but only know it. Already, she found herself thinking about him during the week, being able to recall with startling clarity all that he had said, and his trick of making her look at him while she spoke to him, even though she was showing him some of the children's work.

There was something compelling about him that frightened her, and even if she had wished she could let herself go and say precisely what she thought—as she might have done with her grandfather, or Nat and Lucy—something always held her back, some inner caution that she didn't as yet understand. She only knew she felt safer at a distance from him, mentally and physically. That he had astutely gauged her feelings on this, Josie was sure, for it was shown only too clearly in the teasing light in his eyes when she failed to respond to his friendly overtures.

She was making certain that their acquaintance stayed on a business footing, allowing for no comebacks in their personal relationship—always reminding herself of the reason as to why she was there—to pay back a debt—and that she would have to look for other employment when the time came to close the makeshift school.

Having set her course and refusing to be deviated from it, it was a little disconcerting to find herself in a situation that warranted a personal discussion on a subject she least wanted to bring up—her pay cheque. It was a handsome pay cheque too, and Josie being well versed in the rates of pay in that country, knew she had been grossly overpaid. But worse than this was the fact that no deductions had been made, and she would have felt a little better about it if there had been.

As the pay envelope had been placed on her desk on the Friday morning, she had only to wait until the close of school that day to take the matter up with Kade. By the time the children had left, and he appeared, Josie had worked herself up to a simmering fury. Only too clearly did she recall his words on their third meeting when the proposition was put to her. How he had grandly offered to forget the debt if she accepted the post, and how he had hinted at the remuneration she would receive if he obtained Carella.

Staring down at the cheque in her hand, she felt that it represented a pay-off—for services yet to come—and wanted to tear it up into little bits. So much for his efforts in making her feel a very special person—it was very clever of him, she fumed, and she had almost believed that he meant it. Had he found his softening-up process wasn't working fast enough, and had decided to try hard cash?

When he sauntered in and gave her the usual slow smile that had once had such an effect on her, she found she was actually trembling with rage and could hardly bear to look at him, but she did, and her eyes flashed blue sparks as they clashed with the cool grey ones.

'I think there's been a mistake here,' she said as she held out the cheque for him to see, her voice warning him not to indulge in platitudes.

Barely affording the cheque a glance, Kade raised his left eyebrow as he looked back at her. 'No mistake,' he said firmly. 'It's what I consider the rate for the job.'

Josie drew a deep breath. 'Have you any idea of what a teacher is paid, Mr Boston?' she queried with a glint in her eye.

There was amusement in his eyes as he answered slowly, 'Yes, Miss West, I have—but I still think it's a fair rate for the task you're tackling—with a little aggravation pay added, of course.'

Taking full note of the last remark, Josie thought the word 'aggravation' summed up the situation nicely—in more ways than one. 'I agreed to do the work,' she replied coldly. 'And under the circumstances I don't think it warrants such a salary. I also,' she went on quickly, seeing that he was about to interrupt her, 'see that no deductions have been made. It was agreed that there would be, if I remember rightly,' she challenged.

This brought an answering glint to Kade's eyes, and Josie didn't feel so bad about things. He hadn't liked being reminded about that, she thought. It also looked as if her original thinking as to why she had been paid such a handsome salary was correct. It must be galling for him to find his second ploy hadn't worked either, and that she was not to be bought.

His clipped, almost harsh reply to this told her that he had correctly assessed her thinking. 'I am not in the habit of throwing money away, Miss West—whatever else you choose to think of me—or whatever other interpretation you care to put on it.' He gave a grim nod in acknowledgment of Josie's bright flush at this bald statement. 'I admit I did not make any deduction,' his jaw hardened and his eyes pierced hers. 'For that I apologise. I shall make up for it next month—if that's agreeable?'

The question was shot at Josie, who was still recovering from his earlier attack, and all she could do was to give a small nod of agreement. 'Now, is there anything else you have to discuss with me?' Kade asked abruptly, as if his patience with her was exhausted; and it very probably was, she thought miserably as she tried to concentrate on his last question. There had been something she had wanted to tell him—or ask him—but whatever it was, it had been pushed out of her mind by the turn of events.

When she shook her head dumbly, he said curtly, 'Good; you know where to find me if you've any other queries,' and turning on his heel he strode to the door, leaving Josie in no doubt of the fact that he was an exceedingly angry man.

The door closed with a hard snap, and only by exercising a certain amount of self-control had he refrained from slamming it, surmised Josie as she stared at the closed door in front of her, still partially dazed from the way he had countermanded her challenge. The swift counter-attack had left her floundering, and had made her feel the lowest of the low—not only ungrateful, but positively mean!

Her eyes dimmed with tears as she thrust the cheque into her bag. If only she knew Kade and could trust him—but she didn't. She could only remember that he wanted Carella, and try as she might, she couldn't forget the way he had offered her money for her help in obtaining his goal.

She sighed as she locked her desk, and picking up her bag walked to the door. If only everything had been straightforward from the start, she would willingly have accepted his offer of friendship— and more than that, she conceded miserably, for there was no doubt in her mind that Kade had the power to enslave her heart. Only the memory of what had gone before had saved her heartbreak, she told herself as she climbed into her car, and only too clearly could she see the future should she be foolish enough to play his game. With Carella in his pocket, she would find herself standing outside the gates of paradise clutching a fat cheque, with a smiling Kade directing her to seek other pastures.

At this thought her hand clenched on the car wheel. She was glad she had made him furious with her! He had to learn some time that she wasn't going to be bribed or flattered into bowing to his wishes. In all probability he would fire her now; there were plenty of other qualified teachers to do the work she was doing—and how she wished he would! She was tired of having to weigh up each small incident and place other interpretations on them, and she wanted to be done with skirmishing on the boundaries of cold reasoning. Open war was much to be preferred, as against Kade's type of guerrilla warfare where her every move was checkmated with devastating swiftness. He was so much better at the game than she was, she mused miserably. It would have been fairer if she had been able to read his thoughts as he so obviously. read hers, thus being one step, if not two, in front of her.

CHAPTER SEVEN

THE following Monday, Josie half expected to find a note of dismissal on her desk, and knew a sense of untold relief when she found nothing more incriminating than a terse note from Kade telling her that Maryanne would be leaving half an hour earlier on Tuesdays and Thursdays, to take music lessons at Blue Mount.

Even the bold signature looked intimidating, Josie mused as she studied the short missive, and she knew she hadn't been forgiven for her unspoken thoughts on the matter of the cheque. However, she didn't mind that one bit. Her feelings were still the same, and the longer Kade stayed annoyed with her, the easier it would be to keep him at a distance.

Her relief at not being dismissed far outweighed any other consideration, and told Josie a few things she would rather not have had to admit to herself. Her exact feelings for Kade, for one thing, and how well he had undermined her defences. She had once said that Kade was proud—well, she was proud too, and not for worlds would she allow any hint of her feelings to get through to him. She gulped at the thought of the sort of set-down he would hand out to her should he become aware of her weakness. Ice-cold politeness, or a furious tirade, would be welcome against such an alternative.

Before mid-morning, the news of Maryanne's

coming music lessons formed the major subject of conversation—from that young lady's contribution anyway, and by then the boys were heartily sick of listening to the numerous qualifications her music teacher had attained, and Josie, feeling a little lenient towards the child, for she had had a rough time lately in the adoration stakes, did not call her to order as promptly as she might have done in the past, and allowed her a little more leeway.

However, by the time the morning break was due, even she was tired of the continual accolade attributed to Maryanne's music teacher, who she learnt answered to the name of Miss Hanway, and lived in the nearby township. There was no lack of information on this front, for it appeared that Maryanne had attended a garden party over the weekend at which Miss Hanway had presided as hostess, and apparently taken to Maryanne in a big way, hence the offer of music lessons.

Although the name 'Hanway' echoed a faint prick of suspicion that she had heard it before, Josie made no mental attempt to place it, for she had been away from her home town for a long time, and Maryanne would no doubt very soon fill in the relevant facts without Josie probing. It also occurred to Josie that Kade had probably come to the same conclusion as she had—that his niece was having a thin time of it, and a little extra attention might not come amiss at this stage. Her school reports had shown that the child was making an effort to catch up on her grade—not, Josie suspected, that it was entirely due to the closer supervision she had been subjected to, but a matter of pride, for the boys too had made a promising start, and with a little more effort could well overtake her, but however much Josie wished she could spur them on to make that extra effort, she had to hold her peace and wait for the response to come from the boys themselves. To push them at this stage could be disastrous, and could undo all the slow foundation work she had taken such pains to achieve.

A week later Josie's hopes in this direction were fulfilled, and the boys were given the spur they so badly needed by a chance remark of Maryanne's, as usual on a personal subject, and her one and only topic, her music teacher!

It occurred after a short altercation with the boys about whose turn it was to collect the iced drinks at the morning break period, and as the boys rightly reminded her, it was hers. Maryanne promptly reminded them of her position—and it was not the first time she had brought this ploy into play, only to be sharply rebuked by Josie, but this time the name of her music teacher was introduced to add more weight to her argument. 'Miss Hanway says you ought to be very grateful for having such a chance of schooling,' she reminded the boys haughtily, 'and she says it must be hard for me having to attend as well. Especially as I've been used to private tuition,' she added grandly, with one eye on Josie to see her reaction. 'When it's vacation, Miss Hanway said, she'll be able to give me more time,' persisted Maryanne staunchly, seeing that her earlier remarks had not had the desired effect on either Josie or the boys. 'So I expect I shall only be attending in the mornings.'

This disclosure, however, did have an effect on

the boys, but not quite what Maryanne was hoping for. They stared at her, then looked at Josie with an almost pleading expression that was tinged with a little horror. 'We're not working in the vac, are we, Miss West?' asked Pedro in a hushed voice.

Josie's brows rose while she sought for an answer to the question—which incidentally she didn't know! Kade had said nothing about school holidays, and Josie hadn't realised they were quite so close.

Unwittingly Maryanne came to her aid with a haughty, 'Of course you are. You want to go to the new school when it opens, don't you?' she asked majestically.

Pedro's black eyes opened wide and he looked at Juan, then at Billy, and finding no inspiration there, said indignantly, 'That's not for ages yet!'

'That's as much as you know,' retorted Maryanne triumphantly. 'It's opening after the vacation. Everyone's going there, the old school's closing down.' At the disbelief shown on the face of each child, not to mention Josie's at the calm disclosure, Maryanne added for good measure, 'I heard my uncle talking about it on the phone the other day. He's paying for the school, so there's going to be no hold-up. They're going right ahead, and,' she tacked on, giving Pedro a glare, 'you won't be able to go if you can't spell properly, and that's why you're here!'

'It is also,' intervened Josie smoothly, feeling that Maryanne had held the floor long enough, although she had been grateful for her co-operation earlier, 'the reason you are here too, Maryanne.'

This brought an indignant, 'I'm going to a school for young ladies,' from Maryanne. 'My mommy said so!'

Josie was not sorry to see the end of that day, and as she drove home she thought about Maryanne's disclosure, and wondered why Kade had not mentioned the vacation period before. It did occur to her that perhaps he might have meant to mention it on the Friday, but the ensuing events had pushed it out of his mind. Recalling his fury, Josie shrugged impatiently; she couldn't have it both ways. She had made it clear that theirs was a business relationship, so he was not likely to indulge in social talk with her again. Her brow creased, but it wasn't social chatter—it was fact— and it did affect her. What if she had planned to take a holiday during the vacation? Had he thought of that? she wondered. A few seconds' thought on this produced a certain yes. Of course he had; but she owed him a debt, didn't she, and he would expect her to keep to the arrangement. She also wondered if the boys' parents had made any holiday arrangements, but on second thoughts, knew that Kade would have seen to this too. The men worked for him, and in all probability would have to take time off during the slack periods. Oh yes, she mused bitterly, all would have been taken care of. No doubt he would send her another cryptic note giving her the necessary information when it was time.

In this she was wrong, for Kade did mention the vacation period that following Friday, bluntly stating that the children would be attending class as usual, just that and nothing more, and a fuming

Josie wished fervently that she could insist on taking a couple of weeks off herself, particularly as he seemed to take it for granted that she had not made any plans of her own. Of the new school he made no mention, as if it was none of Josie's business, and this further infuriated her. As the children's teacher she ought to have been put into the picture, but apparently he thought otherwise.

If he had wanted to annoy her he couldn't have found a better way of doing it, and for the first time since their initial acquaintance Josie was made to feel a rank outsider, and it hurt her more than she had bargained for. She had not expected any favours, indeed she had made certain of this by bringing up the matter of the cheque, but she had not expected to find herself snubbed either, for that was how she felt about the school episode. It wouldn't have hurt him to mention the school—or the reason why the children would be working through vacation.

In an effort to push these miserable thoughts out of her mind, Josie concentrated on the new school that according to Maryanne would be ready after the vacation, and wondered if there was any chance of her grandfather's hope that she would obtain a post there being fulfilled. Considering that it was only four months before the opening, it was hardly feasible that they would obtain adequate staff in the allotted time, and that, she thought with a lift of her spirits, might very well turn out in her favour. There was no harm in applying anyway, and this she decided to do without delay.

She was half-way home when the thought struck

her that she had no idea whom to apply to—in fact, apart from the news imparted by Maryanne, she knew absolutely nothing, and her cheerfulness, brought on by hope, vanished in a flash, leaving her feeling even more miserable than before.

At supper that evening a subdued Josie tried to take an interest in her grandfather's enthusiastic comments on the doings of the town social committee. While she listened, her eyes rested on his grey head, and a touch of sadness swept over her, mingled with a feeling of thankfulness that she was back with him, and could now look after him as he had once looked after her. Against this fact everything else paled into insignificance, and Josie scolded herself for her earlier despondency. Something would turn up for her, she was sure.

At this point her grandfather broke into her thoughts with an abrupt, 'Heard about the school?'

Josie started. She had forgotten her grandfather's trick of picking up her trend of thinking, and it struck her that Lucy had not been so far off the mark when she had said Kade was like her grandfather. She swallowed quickly; she didn't want to think about Kade. 'Yes, I heard,' she said quietly, adding carefully, 'Seems it's going to be ready much sooner than anybody thought.'

Her grandfather nodded sagely. 'Boston's doing, of course. Might have been a bit hasty where that man's concerned,' he ruminated slowly. 'Done the town a power of good. If he hadn't stepped in and provided the funds, that school would have been hanging fire for months.' He gave Josie a searching stare. 'You'll be all right there, girl. Got the right person to recommend you, he's not the type to forget a favour.' His eyes wrinkled in thought. ''Sides, he's seen what you can do, and Dan was telling me the other day that Nat and Lucy ain't the only ones who are mighty grateful for your help.'

Josie smiled at this accolade, but the smile didn't reach her eyes, and she wished she could explain just how things were between her and Kade Boston, and the real reason why she was teaching at Blue Mount. As for his recommending her, she just couldn't see that likelihood at all—for one thing, he hadn't mentioned the school to her, and for another, Josie was hardly in a position to ask a favour of him, and her pride would not allow her to even make the attempt—no matter how much she wanted a job at the new school, she would have to do without Kade Boston's help. For a moment or so she was tempted to ask her grandfather if he knew the authority she ought to apply to in order to obtain the job she required, but she only just stopped herself in time. Such a request would sound extremely odd in the light of what he had previously said, and he knew her a little too well for her to risk making up a plausible excuse to cover the request. She sighed inwardly; she would have enough explaining to do when and if she didn't get a post at the school.

To her delight, Lucy turned up later that evening, having begged a lift from her father-in-law on his weekly visit to Carella for the chess game with her grandfather, and soon the two girls were settling down for a chat in the homely kitchen, so as not to distract the men from their mental exertions.

As she listened to Lucy's animated talk, that covered the happenings at the store and small snippets of local gossip, Josie's depression vanished, and she realised how much she had missed Lucy's garrulous but cheerful presence, and almost wished she was back at the store.

When all the news had been given, Lucy sat back and gave Josie a bright expectant look. 'Now it's your turn,' she said happily. 'How's the big romance progressing?'

Josie stared back at her, and for one awful moment she thought that Lucy had got hold of some gossip about Kade and herself, but her next words soon dispelled this fear. 'For goodness' sake! You must have heard something!' pleaded an exasperated Lucy.

'About what?' answered Josie, plainly showing her puzzlement at the question.

Lucy tut-tutted impatiently. 'Josie West, it's a good job you don't work for the papers! As a newshound you'd be a dead loss. Jessica Hanway and Kade Boston, of course!'

Josie's eyebrows raised and she stared at Lucy. So that was why the name Hanway had sounded a bell! 'Wasn't that the girl you were telling me about?' she asked a sad-looking Lucy, whose hopes of collecting a scoop had been so rudely shattered.

Lucy nodded. 'Told you she was a trier, didn't I?' she said gloomily. 'Anyone else I wouldn't mind, I've not forgotten what she did to Mirabelle.' Her brow furrowed. 'Doesn't make sense to me at all, not after that set-down Kade gave her at

that do I was telling you about. Still, it seems she's
wormed her way into Blue Mount now. Quite a
regular visitor she is, and sees that everybody
knows it, too. The town's full of speculation about
it, and half waiting for the news of a wedding.' She
gave Josie a gloomy look 'And you didn't know,'
she accused her.

Managing to bite back a smile at Lucy's obvious
disappointment, Josie said mildly, 'Well, I did
know a Miss Hanway was visiting twice a week to
give Maryanne music lessons, but I'm afraid I
didn't connect the name with the girl you told me
about.'

She would have gone on, but Lucy intervened
with a swift, 'Did you say music lessons?' and without giving Josie a chance to answer she went on,
'So that's how she did it! Well, well! Of all the sly
hussies—and not a word to anyone about the
lessons!' She gave Josie's hand a squeeze. 'I take it
all back, dear, you're an ace reporter,' she told her
happily, for she had got her scoop after all.

Josie smiled at her. 'According to Maryanne,
she's very good,' she commented, although she
doubted if Lucy had heard her, she was too busy
digesting the news Josie had given her.

Lucy started and stared at Josie as if trying to
recall just what she had said, then she had it, and
answered grudgingly, 'Oh, she is; I don't know
how many diplomas she's got. Gives the odd private
lesson now and again, but won't tie herself down.
Too afraid of missing the chance of landing herself
a rich husband.' She scowled as a thought struck
her. 'They say she's pretty expensive and charges
the earth for her fees, but I wouldn't mind betting

she's giving lessons free up at Blue Mount. That way she can kid herself she's a friend of the family—and to hear her talk you'd think she was.'

The conversation then passed on to more mundane matters, and Lucy made a supreme effort to put the previous subject aside for future rumination, but it was plain to see she hadn't quite succeeded, as every now and again she would utter a low, 'Well, well...'

It wasn't until the subject of the new school was brought up that Josie had her full attention, particularly after she had shown doubts on the score of her obtaining employment there, for Lucy, like her grandfather, assumed it was just a matter of course. 'I don't see why you should think it's unlikely,' said Lucy after Josie had explained her thoughts on the matter. 'I've told you before, Kade Boston isn't a man to hold a grudge. If you're right for the work—and you are—did I tell you how pleased Miss Plumstead was with Billy?' she demanded, breaking off in the middle of her theme. 'Well then, you've proved what you can do, and whatever else you think of Kade, he's a fair man. If he's any say in the matter, then I'm sure you'll be offered a job.'

Before sleep claimed her that night, Josie lay thinking of what Lucy had said about Kade being a fair man, and she had to admit the truth of this, where Nat and Lucy and probably everyone else was concerned, but things were different with her. He might have tried to forget the things that were said about her when she first came back home—the very story that she herself had instigated, and insisted should become common knowledge—not realising then how it would affect her future, or indeed happiness. She turned restlessly over on to her side; no matter; she would do it again given the same circumstances. She didn't regret that part of it one bit—just the resulting bitter echoes. For the sake of gaining Carella, Kade had made an effort to gain her confidence, and now that that had failed she was no longer of any interest to him.

Lucy's words still stayed with her, though, and no matter how hard Josie tried to convince herself that Kade wouldn't lift a finger to help her obtain a post at the school, she simply refused to believe it. Deep down, she felt she couldn't bear it if such a thing happened. He knew full well that she needed a job, and but for him would still be at the store—not earning a vast wage, it was true—but earning at least something. She didn't want to believe that he would be petty enough to hold the rumours that were going round the town against her. Not even when she remembered the way he had looked at her when she had approached him that day in an effort to prevent him from worrying her grandfather with the cost of the fencing—or the hidden insinuations behind his words when he spoke of the unlikelihood of her obtaining employment at the new school.

With these thoughts in mind, Josie fell asleep, and not surprisingly dreamed of a tall sunburned man with grey eyes that laughed at her, and whose smile pierced her very being.

CHAPTER EIGHT

ANOTHER fortnight passed and Josie, still clinging to the slender hope that Kade, in spite of the almost frigid atmosphere between them during the end-of-the-week sessions, would recommend her to a post at the new school, found herself looking for signs of a return to their earlier association.

There was now only a week to go before the official school vacation period started, and when Kade gave his now customary curt nod after her report on the week's progress and made no passing comment apart from a stiff, 'You've done well, Miss West,' Josie wanted to scream at him that he needn't be so condescending about it. Not that this would have helped the situation one little bit—if anything, it might have started something Josie least wanted, a head-on collision with him.

It was the news of the party that finally and irrevocably demolished Josie's hopes. Maryanne, always ready to score a glancing blow at her unsympathetic teacher, was her informant on this occasion.

There had, according to the smug Maryanne, been a social gathering the previous evening at Blue Mount, and she innocently inquired why Josie had not been present. Miss Hanway had been there, so had Miss Plumstead, and a few other of the town's dignitaries. 'Miss Plumstead asked after you,' she said, darting a sly glance at Josie to see her reaction. 'She wanted to know why you weren't there. I know, because I heard her ask my uncle.'

'There was no reason why I should have been present,' answered Josie calmly, totally unprepared for Maryanne's next broadside.

'Oh, but you should have been,' rejoined Maryanne gleefully, 'they were discussing the new school, and Miss Hanway's been asked to form a committee. I suppose you don't want to go to the new school, and that's why you weren't asked to the party,' she added suggestively.

Josie's glance left Maryanne's watchful eyes and she concentrated on the exercise book in front of her willing herself not to show the child how much this news had affected her. 'They've probably already got their quota of staff,' she murmured casually, and looking up, met Maryanne's intent gaze. 'I'm a newcomer here, remember, Maryanne,' she added softly.

'No, they haven't,' Maryanne replied swiftly. 'I know they haven't, because I heard Miss Plumstead suggest you to Uncle Kade, but he said you wouldn't be interested.'

'I think it's about time we got down to some work,' interjected Josie quickly before Maryanne could dwell on this highly embarrassing theme any longer. 'Juan, will you read the first four lines from the page I've marked in front of you?'

So the morning progressed, and for Josie it was the longest morning she had known since taking the class, and she longed for the lunch break so that she could be alone with her thoughts.

While she prepared a light lunch for herself and her grandfather, Josie knew she ought to tell her grandfather that she would not be working at the new school. The sooner it was over with the better, but for the life of her she couldn't bring herself to talk about it—not yet. The sense of deep hurt was still with her, and the knowledge that Kade had let her down hurt more than the bald fact that she hadn't even been given the chance of accepting a post. Her only champion, it seemed, was Miss Plumstead, and Josie made a mental note of personally thanking her on the first occasion offered for her kind interest.

It did occur to her that she could go over Kade's head, and visit Miss Plumstead. She needn't go into details, but she could tell her that she was interested, and say something on the lines that there had been some misunderstanding on Mr Boston's part.

All these thoughts went through Josie's mind as she drove back to the school after lunch, but by the time she had turned into the drive at Blue Mount, she knew she would do no such thing. If the project had been financed by anyone else but Kade, it might have been possible; as it was, Josie wouldn't accept a job there now if the whole wretched town went down on their knees and begged her to!

Josie felt much better after this; it wasn't the only school in Texas—although it was the only one near Carella—and it meant she would have to look further afield. She sighed heavily; it also meant she would have to be away all week and home for the weekends—but she'd worry about that later. Right now she had to begin looking for other work. She had ten weeks in which to find herself a position— long enough, surely, for something to come up.

When Josie walked into the schoolroom, the boys were totally engrossed in their favourite topic, cowboy heroes, and she rather envied them their uncomplicated existence as she called them to order. Of Maryanne there was no sign, and a query from Josie to the boys on her apparent disappearance produced the answer that Miss Hanway had collected her, but that she would be back in time for afternoon lessons. This was supplied by Pedro, who sounded very regretful about the last bit, and he wasn't the only one, Josie thought, who would welcome a lesson free of her presence.

Since the arrival of Miss Hanway, Maryanne's work quota had fallen depressingly low, and her interest in the lessons still further. If Josie tried to take her to task on this, she would invariably repeat something Miss Hanway had said about there being plenty of time for her to catch up on her schooling when she went to a 'proper school'. Josie was well aware of the implication behind this barbed remark, but knew it would not help her cause to lose her temper with the child.

Of the boys' work, Josie had no complaints; they had gone ahead in leaps and bounds now that they had a goal to aim for. To be excluded from the new school was not to be contemplated—particularly when it became known that a sports section plus swimming pool had been added to the original plans.

Before long they had outstripped Maryanne, and not unnaturally were impatient to go on to an advanced level before she was ready. This state of affairs should have spurred Maryanne on, and Josie was sure that it would have done had not Miss

Hanway been doing a little spadework in the background.

Only too well could Josie see what was happening, but she was powerless to do anything about it. The child thrived on flattery, and badly missed the attention she had been used to receiving as the only child in the company of adults when accompanying her parents on their various excursions in whatever wilderness they were exploring. With a little perseverance, Josie felt that Maryanne could become a nice child, but not with Miss Hanway carrying on the adulation theme and sympathising with her on the imagined slights she felt she had received from Josie and the boys.

Josie was under no illusion as to why Miss Hanway had attached herself to Maryanne. In a way, she had a lot in common with the boys in Josie's class—they each had a goal to aim at—in Jessica Hanway's case it was Kade. Encouraging Maryanne had given her a foothold at Blue Mount and a reason to visit the ranch at every given opportunity, if possible to bring her into contact with Kade. Josie often wondered if in fact she did see Kade, but at this point would always pull herself up sharply. It was no concern of hers if she did, and in the light of what had happened lately, it certainly looked as if Lucy hadn't been all that far off the mark when she had asked about the 'romance'. Kade must have altered his previous attitude towards the girl, to have not only allowed her to visit the ranch twice a week, ostensibly to give Maryanne music lessons, although Josie suspected he would have seen through that ploy for what it was, but he had given her a seat on the school committee, handing her yet another excuse to seek his company.

Five minutes had elapsed over the time the class should have begun by the time Maryanne, accompanied by Miss Hanway, put in an appearance. A breathless Miss Hanway, handing Josie a huge bunch of bright blue flowers, said brightly, 'I do apologise for making Maryanne late. Kade met us on the way back.'

Josie stared at the flowers, then back at Miss Hanway, failing to understand the reason for the gift and forcing her to give some sort of explanation, that judging by her hesitation she was loth to do. 'Er ... Kade sent them,' she said brightly, and went on hurriedly, 'You won't scold Maryanne, will you? It was entirely my fault.'

Josie didn't think this was worth answering, but she did anyway, with a dry, 'I promise I won't beat her this time, Miss Hanway,' which produced a glint in the other girl's eyes.

The glint became a positive rapier beam when Pedro, who had been studying the bright blue flowers Josie held, suddenly announced, 'Heart's desire.'

'I beg your pardon?' said Jessica Hanway coldly, staring at the boy.

'The flowers,' explained Pedro, completely unabashed. 'It's what they're called.'

'Nonsense!' snapped Jessica sharply, and stared back at Josie, then shrugged her elegant shoulders. 'I thought it was a nice thought of Kade's. I did rather overdo the flower arrangement last evening, and giving them away is better than throwing them away.'

On this back-handed compliment she swept out of the room, leaving Josie clutching the flowers a little tighter than was good for the slender stems.

Seeing that Josie had put the flowers down on a windowsill and not attempted to put them in water, Maryanne solicitously offered to carry out this task for her, telling Josie that she knew where she could find a container for them, and although Josie longed to tell her she could stamp on the wretched flowers for all she cared, she made no objection, but all through the afternoon's lesson the bright blue blooms seemed to leer at her from the other side of the room and she had to will herself not to look at them.

When three-thirty came, and Maryanne requested to be excused earlier, as Miss Hanway had left her some extra work to do, Josie gave a sigh of relief, for she had formed the intention of giving the flowers to Pedro to give to his mother. She daren't give them to Billy to take home to Lucy, for quite apart from the interpretation Lucy might put on the episode, Billy had to go back to the ranch-house for transport back to the town, and the way things were running for Josie at the moment she was sure he would either run into Miss Hanway—or worse, Kade!

It was clear that Pedro was not too sure that he ought to accept the gift, even if, as Josie had intimated, he intended to give them to his mother. He also didn't quite understand why Josie should be so anxious to be rid of them, until a solution hit him and he looked at Josie. 'You get hay fever?' he asked brightly.

Mentally asking to be forgiven, Josie nodded,

and the affair was settled. For Josie as she watched the boy leave the classroom holding the bunch of flowers, it was the end of what had turned out to be the worst day of her life. Not only had her hopes been crushed, but she had had to stomach the added insult of receiving what she could only interpret as a 'sorry' gift from Kade. The fact that he must have known how much he had hurt her made things twice as bad from her point of view, and she couldn't ever remember feeling quite so miserable before, not even when she had craved for affection back in England, and received none.

She was about to turn away from the window from where she had been watching Pedro's progress down the narrow path, when a voice broke into the stillness of the hot afternoon. 'Where are you taking those?' demanded Kade of Pedro.

Josie drew in a deep breath—of all the times for Kade to put in an appearance, it would be now! She hurried out to put in a word in Pedro's defence. 'I gave them to him,' she said quietly. 'He's giving them to his mother.' That was all she said, and her eyes met the grey ones resolutely. He knew now what she thought of his gift, and in a way she was pleased, it-was little enough consolation for her.

'Put them in Miss West's car,' he ordered the worried Pedro, who gladly acceded to this request, and made himself scarce directly afterwards.

Josie turned back into the classroom to collect her bag. She would lose the wretched flowers somewhere on the way back, no matter what, she was not going to keep them.

'Just what was that gesture in aid of?' asked

Kade in a dangerous voice that warned Josie of his mood.

'It wasn't "in aid of" anything,' replied Josie, and deciding to take the coward's way out added, 'I occasionally suffer from hay fever. I was just taking precautions, that's all.'

'Liar,' said Kade softly. 'You were taking precautions all right, though, weren't you?'

Josie's hands clenched on her bag; all right, if he wanted a fight he could have one; she owed him nothing now. 'Very well,' she spat out at him. 'If you must know I resent receiving charity, well-meant or otherwise.'

'Thank you,' he grated out harshly, now as furious as she was. 'I suppose it's only your kinfolk you accept charity from, is it?' he added thinly.

Josie went white at the barbed insinuation and looked away quickly, not being able to bear looking at him, or showing him how much the remark had hurt. 'I'm sorry,' she said quietly, 'I didn't mean to offend you.' She was too weary to fight him and only wanted him to go. She couldn't blame him for something she had started herself.

There was a moment's silence before he spoke again, then he said, 'I guess I owe you an apology, too.'

He could have been apologising for letting her down over the new school, but Josie knew better. 'There's no need to apologise, Mr Boston. It's the truth, isn't it?' she answered wearily with a shrug of her slim shoulders, still refusing to look at him.

At the quick indrawn breath he took, she knew he was furious again, and quickly changed the subject in order to end this embarrassing interlude.

'Pedro needs another pair of plimsolls,' she remarked as casually as she was able. 'I noticed he'd worn a hole in the ones he's wearing.'

She glanced quickly back at Kade as she said this and saw that he had not liked the way she had abruptly curtailed any further discussion on personal lines. He studied her silently for a second or two, and Josie, taking the keys out of her bag, locked her desk, giving him a broad hint that she wanted to be off.

'One day, Josie West, you're going to tell me what really happened,' he drawled meaningly, then as if it were an afterthought, added, 'I'll see Pedro gets those plimsolls.'

Josie watched his broad back as he temporarily blocked out the light from the window he passed as he walked down the path and out of her view. She closed her eyes; there was no mistaking the resolve in his voice—like everything else about Kade Boston, he was a man of his word. Why should he bother anyway? Was he telling her he didn't believe the rumours? She shook her head dumbly. He believed them all right—he must have done to have said what he did earlier. Was he curious to know what she had done with the money she had supposedly taken from her grandfather? She gave a small nod at this thought; that would be like Kade Boston too. He wouldn't accept that there were some things that were private.

Tears pricked Josie's eyes as she walked to the schoolroom door. The gift of the flowers showed that he was about to resume friendly relations with her, perhaps intimating that a school job would be hers if she played along with him, and if it hadn't been for that one unguarded slip of his, she might well have fallen into the trap.

With an impatient shake of the head, she shook away the wetness gathering in her eyes. She had not thought that she would welcome the fact that she had not been recommended for a post at the new school, but now she thanked providence that she owed Kade Boston nothing. She bit her lip—well, there was still that wretched fencing, but if she was careful with the housekeeping, she could put aside her next two months' salary and send it back to Kade after she had left his employment. He wouldn't like that one bit, but Josie had no other choice. At least she had stuck to her side of the bargain, and he would have to accept it.

The week the vacation started, Josie found herself devoutly hoping Maryanne was successful in gaining Kade's permission to skip the afternoon lessons, thus enabling her to receive the promised extra music lessons from Jessica Hanway.

Her expectation of finding a note in her desk from Kade advising her of this was soon dashed by the absence of any such missive, and a very sulky Maryanne. To make matters worse, the boys unkindly remarked on the fact that Maryanne wouldn't be attending the afternoon class, when it was patently obvious that the extra coaching she had boasted about the previous week would not be forthcoming, and Josie was hard put to it not to bang their heads together. In all fairness she could not blame the boys for getting a little of their own back, for Maryanne's behaviour towards them in the previous weeks had left much to be desired.

Josie soon found that a belligerent Maryanne was ten times worse to cope with than a bored Maryanne, and most of her time that morning was spent in settling disputes that broke out between her and the boys with depressing regularity, and had nothing to do with the lesson on hand.

This, Josie surmised, would have been the kind of tactic employed by Maryanne during her stay at the local school, and she could well understand the necessity of her early removal, as Kade had said, for the good of the school.

When the boys ignored her petty but infuriating interruptions—such as . . . she couldn't find her pen —was that Pedro's own pen he was using, or had he borrowed hers and if he had, would he please stop chewing the end of it? being just one of them, and Maryanne was forced to adopt another tactic. This time she took an interest in the boys' work, and did not attempt to do any herself, and was soon successful in putting them off their concentration.

Spotting this move, she moved the child's desk so that she could no longer overlook any of the boys work, and placed her in solitary splendour at the back of the class. When Maryanne complained bitterly of the inferior position she had been allocated, Josie moved her forward and the boys' desks back. This delighted the boys, but did nothing for the worsening relationship between Josie and Maryanne.

By the end of that day, Josie seriously considered seeking Kade's help by requesting that Maryanne be allowed to take the time off for the extra music lessons. It was plain that the child did not intend to settle down in class, and very soon the boys' work would deteriorate, and no matter how hard they tried, the continual distractions were bound to affect them.

Josie never knew what actually did happen to bring the situation back to normal, for the next day, to her surprise and needless to say, relief, Maryanne was a model pupil; so much so that Josie reshuffled the desks back to their original positions, bringing Maryanne back into the fold.

When the child attended the afternoon class as well, Josie's puzzlement grew, for she had been convinced that Maryanne had somehow persuaded Kade to let her off the afternoon lessons. However, this apparently was not so, and Josie failed to see what objection Kade could have to the child taking the extra coaching offered by the solicitous Miss Hanway.

It did occur to Josie that perhaps Jessica Hanway had overstepped her welcome at Blue Mount, but she thought this was unlikely. She must have inveigled herself pretty deeply into the household if she had got to the flower arranging stage for the social occasions. Another reason presented itself, and this was more than a probability—if Jessica's time at Blue Mount was taken up by her adoring pupil, Kade would have to take second place—and as Kade was not the kind of man to even consider such a state of affairs, Maryanne's hopes had been non-runners from the start.

Josie sighed. There was no doubt about it, she had certainly earned the extra pay, as far as the aggravation rate was concerned, certainly, for it was she who had had to bear the whiplash of his decision.

Whatever pressure had been brought to bear on Maryanne's behaviour would not, Josie was convinced, last long. Although she was attentive enough, there was a look in her eyes that suggested mischief-making, particularly when they rested on Josie. Altogether it was an extremely uneasy period, not unlike the lull before a storm, and far more wearying on Josie's nerves than an out-and-out row might have been.

Surprisingly, it was Jessica Hanway who inadvertently exposed the reason for Maryanne's impeccable conduct, and the ensuing events must have given her cause for regret, for the trouble that Josie had sensed brewing, and was now about to be released on her, had a boomerang effect on the unsuspecting Miss Hanway.

As it was Tuesday, it was the day for Maryanne's music lesson, for although the extra coaching had not been permitted, the earlier arrangement still stood, and Miss Hanway, not waiting for Maryanne to put in an appearance at the ranch-house, had walked to the school to collect her. It was not the first time she had done this, and Josie had felt that it was her way of showing Josie that her authority over the child was over for the day, and that she was now in command.

On this particular day, she arrived much earlier than the given time, and Josie, in appreciation for Maryanne's good behaviour, did not hesitate in waiving aside the time factor and told Maryanne she could go. Maryanne, however, insisted on finishing her lesson, and it proved her undoing.

With a proprietorial expression on her face, Jessica Hanway seated herself next to Maryanne and watched her laboriously copy out the last few lines of the given lesson, remarking after noticing that she was using a ballpoint pen, 'Where's the pen I gave you, dear?'

Bending closer to her work, Maryanne muttered that she had lost it somewhere.

'Lost it?' repeated a shocked Miss Hanway. 'Where—here?' Her gaze swept over the boys and rested on Miguel, who like the rest of the class was completely engrossed in the same task as Maryanne. She walked over to his desk, then glanced up at Josie. 'This boy is a thief,' she announced baldly. 'You've just heard what Maryanne said, and look at the pen he's using. Surely you must have known Maryanne had lost hers. It's hardly the sort of pen he would own, is it?' she demanded scathingly.

In point of fact, Josie had not heard what Maryanne had said, or indeed had had any indication of such an event, and she looked up in surprise from the work she was doing, that of marking the children's morning exercises. Her look went from Jessica Hanway's accusing finger at Miguel, to the pen he was holding. It looked an expensive pen, probably silver, and Josie had to admit that it was hardly likely that Miguel would own it. On the other hand, Miguel was not a thief, and he had not had the pen that morning, Josie was sure.

'Miguel, where did you get that pen?' Josie asked the trembling boy.

Miguel dropped the pen as if it were red-hot, then looked directly at Maryanne, who seemed to be concentrating on anything but the boy, and as he saw this, his small jaw squared and he said, 'She gave it to me.'

'She', obviously being Maryanne, made an attempt at denial. 'He's lying,' waded in Jessica, coming to Maryanne's assistance. 'I only gave it to her yesterday. She wouldn't have given it to him.'

Josie sighed inwardly. Where Maryanne was concerned no such supposition was justified. The child had her own rules of conduct, and might even have given Miguel the pen to cause trouble. It was a sad but true fact that Josie preferred to believe Miguel's explanation, whatever it was, to Maryanne's denial.

As if he sensed this, Miguel's black eyes stared pleadingly at Josie. 'She did give it to me,' he said, then swallowed hard as if the next part of his explanation was the hard part, for he looked away from Josie's questioning eyes to the floor. 'She gave it to me so that I wouldn't tell you I saw her with your bag at the break period. She took it when you went to get the drinks. The others were talking, and they didn't see,' he added lamely, and stared back defiantly at Maryanne.

'You promised!' hissed Maryanne, too intent on unleashing her fury on Miguel to realise what she had said.

Perplexed, Josie stared from him to Maryanne, but before she could ascertain the truth of this, Jessica again flew to her prodigy's assistance. 'As if Maryanne would do such a thing! The boy's just thought that up to cover the fact that he took the pen,' she said coldly.

Josie continued looking at Maryanne. 'What did

you want with my bag, Maryanne?' she asked quietly.

'Hell!' exploded Jessica. 'It's obvious whose side you're on! Don't bother to answer, Maryanne,' she commanded haughtily.

'Answer the question, Maryanne,' Kade ordered, and all eyes went to him as he stood just inside the schoolroom door.

'Ah, Kade!' sighed the triumphant Jessica. 'Now we shall get to the bottom of things. Don't worry, Maryanne, your uncle will soon settle this.'

Of this Maryanne had no doubt, and her thin shoulders drooped despondently on the thought, and she took refuge in tears.

'Well, I'm waiting,' drawled Kade, showing her that tears were of no avail, and that he meant to have an answer.

Maryanne shook her head blindly, and the volume of tears increased at an alarming rate. Josie felt that things had gone far enough, and glanced at Kade, who seemed unperturbed by the emotion his niece was displaying. 'Perhaps she was curious to know what was in the handbag,' she suggested mildly. 'Little girls are curious, you know, and I hardly think it warrants the child getting so upset. I think it would be better if we left it at that,' she added firmly.

Jessica, deciding it was about time she added her sentiments, nodded her head at this, adding a cynical, 'If Maryanne has done such a thing, which frankly I don't believe.'

Neither of these points of view had any effect on Kade, whose eyes were still on the sobbing Maryanne. 'Would you please check the contents of your bag, Miss West?' he requested of Josie. 'It's obvious that my niece is unable to refute the charge. It may, as you say, have only been curiosity, but under the circumstances I would like you to ascertain that nothing is missing.'

Josie had no choice but to do as he had bid. She knew he was right, and if her deduction had been correct, and the child had been curious, then no harm would have been done, and would only warrant a lecture in the very near future for the miserable Maryanne.

Opening the bag, she quickly checked the contents. All seemed to be there, and she was about to report this fact when her searching fingers encountered a cold object that slithered from her touch and buried itself deeper within the bag.

Her eyes opened wide in horror as she dropped the bag on to the desk where it fell with a dull thud, and she took an involuntary step backwards, terrified that the thing the bag contained would escape. She was not in the habit of fainting, but she came very close to it at that moment. Kade, taking two swift strides, was beside her, and placing a chair behind her, made her sit down.

Chalk-white, Josie closed her eyes in an effort to blot out the sight and feel of that thing. She had a horror of snakes, poisonous or otherwise. She felt Kade's strong fingers bite into her shoulder blades as he forced her head between her knees and barked out for someone to get her a glass of water.

Josie wanted to say she didn't want any water. If she had tried to swallow it would have choked her, for her throat had constricted with shock and for a second or two she was unable to speak.

A few seconds later she felt able to sit back and accept the glass Kade held out to her, and watched with a kind of fascinated horror while he picked up her bag and sought to identify the cause of her terror. 'Don't put your hand in,' she said sharply as she saw him about to do this, but he took no notice and a few seconds later he found what he was look-ing-for and began to remove it from the bag.

Unable to watch, Josie turned away, feeling sick, and although she heard him ask her to look at what was in his hand, she shivered uncontrollably, and shook her head mutely. When the request was repeated, this time more firmly, she still could not comply. 'J-just g-get rid of it,' she got out weakly.

She heard Kade give a loud sigh, then he said mildly, 'It's not a snake, Miss West, it's a sand lizard and perfectly harmless, I can assure you.'

Josie clenched her hands tightly round the glass she was holding in an effort to stop them trem-bling, and a little of the water spilled over into her lap, but she was not aware of this. Sand lizard or not, to Josie it was a snake. Lizards had legs, and this thing hadn't, and although she was sure Kade knew what he was talking about, to her way of thinking it was a snake that was called a sand lizard, she just didn't want to know the ins and outs of whether it was harmless or not, she just wanted it out of her proximity.

Still refusing to look at the creature in Kade's hand, she heard him order Pedro to take the lizard out, in a resigned voice that told Josie that he'd like to shake her for her obstinate refusal to listen to what he had hoped had been a calming state-ment.

Only when she heard the schoolroom door close behind Pedro did she turn back to meet Kade's watching eyes, and she flushed as she acknowledged his softly drawled, 'You've a lot to learn, Miss West.'

Although the words were meant for her ears alone, Maryanne must have caught the drift of them, for she gave a high-pitched giggle, partially, Josie suspected, in relief at her let-off, for only she could have placed the creature in her bag.

Kade swung round and looked at the gleeful Maryanne. 'I don't know why you should find the situation funny, my girl. Let's hope you feel the same way about things after we've had a little talk. Go straight to your room, and stay there until I send for you,' he commanded.

Maryanne's amusement left her, and she started to cry again, louder this time than before. 'And stop that snivelling,' Kade ordered. 'It didn't work before, and it's not going to work now.'

'Don't be too cross with her, Kade,' interceded Jessica. 'It wasn't such a bad thing she did. The creature was harmless,' she flung Josie a disdainful look. 'Anyone else would have known it was, and it certainly wasn't worth the fuss Miss West made of it. Why, I remember my mother telling me once that she played the same trick on her teacher when she was young.'

Kade's narrowed eyes rested on her. 'You wouldn't by any chance have mentioned this to Maryanne, would you?' he asked casually.

Jessica shrugged offhandedly, 'I might have done —to be honest, I'm not sure,' she said quickly, but Josie was sure, and so apparently was Kade, for as she placed a comforting arm around the still sobbing Maryanne and said soothingly, 'Come on, dear, I'll go back with you,' he barked out authoritatively, 'She knows the way, Miss Hanway, and I should be obliged if you would wait outside for a few minutes. I want to have a word with you.'

Jessica blanched at the cold directive, and Josie knew a spurt of surprise that he had called her 'Miss Hanway', as she had presumed that they were on christian name terms. 'Very well,' she answered, attempting to give him a coy smile that didn't quite come off and appeared rather as a grimace.

Maryanne was now denied her champion, and, astute enough to realise this, turned furiously on Josie. 'It's all your fault!' she shouted at her. 'I'm glad the lizard frightened you. It was your fault I couldn't have extra music lessons,' she sobbed hysterically. 'Miss Hanway said how you were jealous of her, and Uncle Kade always listened to you, and not to her, even though she told him about you taking your grandfather's money.'

'Maryanne!' the name was thundered out by a furious Kade. 'One more word, and that talk will turn to a beating—as it is, I can't even promise a talk. You'll apologise to Miss West, do you hear?'

Maryanne heard, but she had no intention of complying with the order, and rushed out of the door on her way back to the ranch-house.

For a few seconds there was a pregnant silence in the schoolroom, and a white-faced Josie gazed bleakly at the boys who had been unfortunate enough to witness the disturbing, if not distressing events of that afternoon. She saw with a touch of sadness how they had shrunk into their seats, as if willing themselves elsewhere, and it occurred to her that Maryanne's last spiteful outburst had not come as a surprise to them—so they too had known, she thought wearily.

Following her look, Kade interpreted her thoughts, and gave the boys their marching orders, that they were only too ready to receive, and with an agility that had to be seen to be believed, they made their departure.

With a look that plainly said, 'Wait', Kade went outside to have his promised talk with the by now extremely apprehensive Jessica Hanway, for she must have heard Maryanne's last broadside in her defence, and it would not have done her cause much good.

With legs that felt like jelly, Josie sank down on to the chair again. She had no choice but to do exactly as Kade had silently ordered her to do. She badly needed a breathing space and was devoutly grateful she would not be within hearing range of whatever it was that Kade had to say to Jessica Hanway.

Josie had a nasty feeling that she was the next one on the list, and couldn't honestly blame Kade if he did go for her. If she hadn't been so weak-minded and had managed to control her revulsion at the sight of that creature. none of this would have happened and the incident would have been passed off as a childish prank on Maryanne's part without the subsequent embarrassment.

She was staring down at her hands when he came back into the schoolroom, and she glanced up at him briefly, then down at her hands again, unable to hold his glance. 'Don't be too hard on Maryanne,' she said in a low voice. 'Miss Hanway was right when she said I oughtn't to have made such a fuss.' She took a deep breath. 'Under the circumstances, I think it would be better if you found someone else to take over the job.' She did look up then, and met his narrowed gaze. 'I would prefer you do so,' she added quietly.

'Chickening out?' he drawled sarcastically, then his voice hardened. 'And if I refuse to release you from the bargain?' he asked harshly.

Josie stiffened. He meant to collect that debt, didn't he? Even after what had happened; oh, he was hard all right, it was obvious he didn't fancy looking for a replacement during the vacation. 'There's lots of teachers that take jobs during the vacation,' she said firmly, refusing to lose her temper. 'You'd only have to advertise.'

'I like the one I've got,' he countermanded maddeningly.

Josie clenched her teeth; there were several ways one could take that statement, she thought, if one was looking for compliments, that was, but she wasn't, and she was pretty certain why he was insisting on keeping her. She lived at Carella, and he wanted Carella—it was simple really.

When he saw that she had no intention of answering his dubious compliment, he suddenly barked at her, 'Why are you throwing in the towel? Because of Maryanne—or what she said before she took off in a paddy?'

Josie stood up quickly. This was getting a little too personal for her liking. 'Let's say I'm chickening out,' she snapped, adding as brightly as she was able to, 'You've seen what a coward I am, so I'm sure you'll understand.' She turned swiftly back towards her desk and picked up her bag, only just managing to repress a shiver as she touched it. Kade might not be through, but she was; she had taken about all she could take.

She did not hear him move towards her, only felt the strength of his fingers bite into her arms as he swung her round to face him. His eyes went slowly and deliberately over her features, and Josie was too surprised to attempt to move out of his hold, not that she could have done so if she had tried. 'The hell of it is, I don't understand,' he bit out furiously, 'but make no mistake, I intend to find out!' He bent his head swiftly and kissed her hard on the mouth.

'That,' he said grimly when he at last released her, 'is something on account. Do you remember asking me once if I always got what I wanted?' he asked the partially shocked Josie. 'And my reply? Well, where you're concerned there's a hell of a lot of things I want, but first things first. You stay on here—you gave me your word and I'm keeping you to it. If you're not here tomorrow I shall pay your grandfather a visit. I wonder if he knows the real reason why you accepted the job?' he said softly but meaningly.

Josie drew in a shuddering breath. It was blackmail! And although she had half expected something of this nature to happen, she found she couldn't really believe it was happening. Did one acre of land mean so much to him? If so, it might be as well to advise her grandfather to sell up and be done with it. She swallowed. 'How much are you offering for Carella?' she asked wearily.

He drew in a quick breath, and Josie knew he was furious. He gripped her arm again, and she winced at the touch. 'If I thought,' he grated, 'that you were about to make a bargain with me——' He was silent for a second, then when he spoke again his voice was softer yet somehow more determined than before. 'Forget Carella,' he advised her. 'That side of it has already been taken care of.'

CHAPTER NINE

'You can forget Carella.' The words pounded through Josie's brain as she drove home after her shattering encounter with Kade.

As for the kiss, she simply refused to even acknowledge it, even in her thoughts. To her, it was just one more shock to add to the previous one, and as she wished to put the lizard episode out of her mind, so too did she want to forget the kiss.

Concentrating on what he had said about Carella was far safer than recalling the hard pressure of his lips on hers. At this thought Josie swerved to avoid running into a ditch. No, she must think about Carella, nothing else mattered.

Her brow creased in an effort to recall his exact words. Carella had been taken care of—or words to that effect—and Kade was not a man to make idle statements. Did that mean that he had come to some arrangement with her grandfather? If so, why hadn't her grandfather mentioned it to her? Her frown deepened; she knew he was worried about her trying to do too much. Carella was a large house, and the fact that she was tackling the garden as well had not gone unnoticed by him.

Josie sighed and shook her head; she just couldn't see him going over her head, it wasn't like him; especially since she had asked him not to sell up.

By the time Josie arrived home, she had got no

further with her queries; she was more perplexed, if anything, and knew she would have to wait until an opportunity presented itself to enable her to tackle her grandfather about it. To ask straight out would be bound to bring a few facts to light, and Josie preferred things as they were.

It was all very well telling herself to wait and try to forget Kade's words, or entertain the hope that for once he hadn't meant what he had said, and was trying to bamboozle her into co-operating, not only with the children's schooling, but more importantly with helping him gain Carella.

As Josie walked up the drive to the house, she stopped in mid-stride as a thought struck her. She had offered him assistance, hadn't she?—or at least shown him she was willing to co-operate on the last score, but it hadn't gone down at all well considering his furious reaction. So much, she thought bitterly, for her decision to put the matter out of her mind. She couldn't, and before long the memory of that devastating kiss would awaken yearnings she had managed to keep at bay so successfully until now.

What she needed was a change of scenery, and on this thought she decided to pay Lucy a return visit that evening. If anyone could make her forget her troubles, Lucy could.

After clearing away the remains of their evening meal, Josie duly set out on her visit to Lucy. As she made the journey, walking slowly to savour the evening air, she thought of her grandfather's nod of approval when apprised of her destination. She knew he was still a little peeved that none of the townsfolk had made the expected calls to make her acquaintance, and had eventually come to accept her hurriedly thought up explanation that they were giving her time to settle down. How long this excuse would last, Josie had no idea, but it had served to allay his suspicions, for the time being anyway.

On finding Josie on her doorstep, Lucy practically fell on her, and dragged her into the sitting-room. 'Am I glad to see you!' she enthused. 'Nat's taken the kids to see the new school. It's considered the local show,' she grinned. 'I said I'd wait until the paths were completed, I don't fancy leaving my dainty footprint in a patch of damp cement.'

Josie grinned, and felt better already, and soon the talk continued on more general lines, and inevitably landed up at Blue Mount. Josie had foreseen this, of course, and had guessed that Lucy would demand to know what had actually happened between Kade and Jessica Hanway, for she would have got some of it from Billy, who had been present. Not being in the vicinity, Josie would be unable to fill this particular gap in for her, and she thought with an inward smile that she was going to let Lucy down again.

However, to Josie's surprise no such question was asked, and when Lucy did not refer to the lizard episode Josie came to the conclusion that Billy had not mentioned what had happened that day at school. She was grateful for this, and wondered if Kade had had anything to do with it, but didn't see how he could have done, for the boys had taken off pretty quickly when given the word.

Lucy did know that Jessica Hanway had ceased visiting Blue Mount. 'Guessed there was something up,' she told Josie. 'Mrs Carver met her on the way back from school. She'd done me a favour by fetching my two back at the same time,' she enlightened Josie. 'Well, was she in a paddy—er—Jessica, I mean,' she grinned. 'Said she'd finished going up to Blue Mount, and took the trouble to explain to Mrs Carver that she went up there to give Miss Boston music lessons, but the child simply wasn't musical. And that was the first time she had mentioned what she was going up there for. So all her putting-on of airs and letting everyone know she was visiting there came to nothing. If you ask me,' she confided to Josie, 'she overstepped the mark. Kade's not one to stand on ceremony over things like that. I couldn't understand why she was given the job in the first place. Of course, if the child asked for her, I suppose there wasn't much he could do about it,' she mused thoughtfully.

Josie listened but said nothing, but it did occur to her that it would be nice if some other subject could be discussed, in fact any other subject but Blue Mount.

'She's making sure she gets her story in first,' went on Lucy, unaware of Josie's thoughts. 'Not that Kade would say anything, he's too much of a gentleman for that.'

Again Josie kept her thoughts to herself; a gentleman he might be, until things didn't go his way—then he could be positively ungentlemanly. Take the way he had used blackmail to make her toe the line—and not only blackmail, she thought as she remembered the way he had kissed her, as if putting his stamp on her. At this thought she felt her face go hot, and hastily picked up a cardigan

Lucy was knitting for one of her daughters, and commented on the intricate pattern, successfully turning Lucy's attention away from the previous subject.

On the way home she wondered where the idea of Kade's kiss putting a seal on her had come from. From what she knew of him it didn't make sense, unless he was peeved because his smiles hadn't enslaved her. For they had been deliberate, she knew this, and they had almost worked. It was probably the first time, she thought ruefully, that he hadn't impressed a female, and it must have rankled. She almost sighed with relief at this thought, so it made sense after all, and was a far more comfortable answer than the one that had been hovering at the back of her mind since he had kissed her.

Having got that little worry off her mind, she was rather dismayed to hear her grandfather's news when she arrived back at Carella.

'Dan called,' he said with an air of suppressing some important news. 'There's a shindig at the town hall on Friday. Seems the Mayor's come up with the idea of giving a party for Kade—thinks it's a good way of saying "thanks" for the school.'

Josie eyed him warily. If he was going to suggest she should go, then she would have to make some excuse, for she had no intention of going to any party that Kade was attending—not at this stage of their relationship, if it could be called such. Joseph went on. 'They've asked me to do the speech,' he said, clearing his throat loudly, showing Josie that he was pleased, 'me being the oldest member of the committee, that is.'

Josie swallowed. This was worse than she had imagined. What sort of a speech would he give when he heard that his niece had not been recommended for a post at the new school? She blinked; it didn't bear thinking about. One thing was very clear, and that was that he would expect her to accompany him, and no amount of excuses would serve to cover her absence.

It was also clear that Josie could no longer put off telling him that she would not be included in the staff. Trying to inject a careless note into her voice, she said brightly, 'Well, that's nice of them. I'm sure you'll do them proud, even though I've failed to get a place at the school,' holding her breath for his reaction to this news.

He stared at her, and the familiar scowl came over his weatherbeaten face, and Josie sighed inwardly. 'Who said so?' he demanded.

Josie linked an arm in his. 'Well, I did mean to warn you that it wasn't as cut and dried as you thought it was going to be,' she said soothingly. 'I was trained in England, remember, and couldn't expect to take precedence over teachers trained here.' It sounded reasonable, she thought, and hoped her grandfather would think so too.

'You might have been trained in England, but you're American,' he snorted. 'Can't see that that's anything to do with it. You've as much right to a job as anybody else.'

Josie gave a small sigh at this. 'Gramps, you're biased,' she scolded mildly. 'I'm not worried about it' she lied. 'There'll be other opportunities, you'll see. I haven't really started looking yet.'

'Guess I'll have a word with Boston,' muttered her grandfather darkly. 'Seems he forgot you'd be looking for a job when the new school opened.'

'Don't you dare!' Josie got out swiftly, fervently

hoping the panic she felt at this news hadn't shown in her voice. 'Look, Gramps,' she said, managing to inject a note of calm into her words, 'can't you see that that's the last thing I want? I want to be independent. I'm not afraid of competition. I want to get work on my qualifications, and not on someone else's say-so. I'd never feel I'd earned my place, you see,' she ended lamely, and giving her grandfather a quick glance saw that he was having trouble accepting this explanation. 'All right,' she went on wearily, 'call it pride if you like, and if it is, then I can't help it. I must have inherited it from you anyway.' Her eyes met the faded blue ones resolutely. 'I thought you'd understand,' she added sorrowfully.

Joseph squeezed her hand, reacting in the way that Josie had hoped he would. 'Okay, girl,' he said gruffly. 'They're fine sentiments, and I guess we always did have more pride than was good for us.'

Nothing more was said, and Josie was thankful that she had been able to make him understand, but she didn't see the puzzled look he sent her that rested on her bowed head as she stared at her clenched hands.

Josie went back to Blue Mount the next morning, and half expected to find Kade waiting for her to put in an appearance. However, when she arrived at the school, she found the boys and an extremely subdued Maryanne waiting for her. Apart from Maryanne's hastily mumbled, 'Sorry, Miss West,' all was as normal, and although Kade did not put in an appearance, Josie was almost certain that he was well aware of the fact that she was in attendance.

The rest of that week passed by without a hint of the earlier disturbance. For the first time, Josie learned what it was like having a class of not only interested pupils, but happy pupils. She marvelled at the change in Maryanne, and was curious to know how Kade had worked the miracle. Maryanne not only gave fervent attention to her lessons, but went out of her way to please the boys as well, and practically insisted on fetching the drinks at the break periods each day. All this was accepted with the natural resilience that children have; they did not question the fact that Maryanne had turned over a new leaf, or looked for what might be termed as 'the catch' in her exemplary behaviour, although they might have been forgiven if they had.

Friday, the day Josie was secretly dreading, came at last. It was not only Kade's expected appearance at the close of school that was causing her apprehension, but the party that was being given in his honour at the town hall that evening, and she wondered if he would make any mention of the party during his visit. She fervently hoped that he wouldn't, for she was still working on an excuse to give her grandfather as to why she couldn't attend, but she knew with gloomy certainty that she was not going to be allowed to get out of it. However, Kade was not to know that her grandfather had been elected to give the speech that night, and if Josie had to attend, it ought to be possible to keep out of Kade's way. There was bound to be a lot of folk at that party, and she could see no difficulty in avoiding him. As long as her grand-father knew she was there, that was all that mattered, and as Dan would be there too, she had no doubt that he would keep her grandfather company, giving her ample opportunity to fade into the background.

As long as she could keep the conversation on purely scholastic lines, all would be well, she told herself on the way to school that morning. On the other hand, if Kade did ask her if she was going, and she had to answer yes, then she wouldn't put it past him to seek her out—and if she happened to be with her grandfather—— She swallowed; why couldn't she have a tiny accident, such as breaking her leg? She wouldn't have to worry then what might or might not happen.

Josie might have known that she wasn't going to be given a chance either of getting out of the party or of manipulating the conversation she thought she was going to have with Kade later, for a cheerfully given message from Kade relayed by Maryanne that, 'Uncle Kade said he'll see you tonight,' ended all further speculation on Josie's part.

For the rest of that day, her mind was busy thinking up ways of keeping her grandfather and Kade apart. On no account must she give her grandfather a chance of a word alone with Kade, for she was certain that he would take the opportunity of tackling Kade and reminding him that she was looking for a job, in which event, she thought miserably, she would be looking for a job a great deal sooner than either of them had anticipated!

If it only concerned the question of a job for her, Josie might have actually looked forward to the confrontation between Kade and her grandfather. She had wanted to leave Blue Mount anyway, but it wouldn't stop at that. She was no longer sure of what Kade was up to; at one time she had thought he was using her to obtain Carella, now it seemed he had found some other way of obtaining his goal, and Josie was sure that her grandfather was as unenlightened as she was on the method he had decided to use. Not that her grandfather had any inkling of what was going on, and Josie would have hated him to find out. The way Kade would have told it, it would have looked as if she had become Kade's accomplice in pushing him out of his home, in spite of her plea to him to try and keep the house and what was left of the land.

With these thoughts at the back of her mind, Josie's nerves were far from calm when Dan collected them to take them to the town hall. To make matters worse from her point of view, her grandfather had insisted on an early arrival. It wouldn't do, he had said, for the guest to arrive before they did, as it was planned to give the thank-you speech to Kade on his arrival at the hall.

On hearing this, Josie hoped Kade would put in a late appearance; that way she could enjoy at least part of the evening, and with any luck her grandfather would depart soon afterwards. Social occasions had never been his forte, and with his duty done, he would be anxious to get back home and rid himself of the stiff collar and equally uncomfortable best suit that Josie had searched out for him and pressed in readiness for the occasion.

As for her dress, she had wanted to wear an ordinary one, as she saw no occasion for her to dress up. In any case, she didn't possess a dress that might be termed evening wear, only a long black velvet skirt that could pass muster as such if the situation warranted it—and, according to her grandfather—it did, and the exasperated Josie had to search around for a suitable blouse to go with it, eventually coming up with a white long-sleeved one that received her grandfather's approval.

It was as if Kade had sensed her wish that he should make a late appearance, for like everything else that Josie had hoped for where he was concerned, he disappointed her, and arrived ten minutes or so after them.

Her prediction that there would be a crowd at the party was fulfilled however, and very soon after her grandfather had welcomed him on behalf of the town committee, and conveyed their thanks to him for his generosity in supplying them with a new school, Kade was surrounded by a small crowd of the grateful townsfolk.

From her position on the fringes of the gathering, Josie took good care to keep out of range of those eagle eyes of his, and with a cover of at least a dozen people in front of her she was able to watch him, yet not be seen. In particular, she kept an eye on her grandfather, hovering on the outskirts of the nearest group to Kade, and saw with a certain amount of relief that Dan had claimed his attention, for she had a nasty suspicion that her grandfather was waiting for a chance to have a private word with Kade when and where the occasion offered.

Her glance left her grandfather and rested on Kade again. He was listening to something an elderly lady was saying, and her heart jerked treacherously as she saw him smile. No matter how much she disliked his methods in getting what he wanted, she had to admit he was an extremely handsome man. Wearing a tuxedo, he stood way out from the crowd, although he was not the only one to wear evening dress. The Mayor, for one, had honoured the occasion by wearing an evening suit, and needless to say, Jessica had taken the opportunity of attiring herself in a dreamy gossamer dress in the classical style, and Josie had to admit the style suited her dark sensuous good looks.

As she watched Jessica talking to a small group of people, and keeping a hopeful eye in Kade's direction, Josie marvelled that Kade hadn't been attracted. She had everything in her favour—she was not only lovely, but was clever, too. Her only fault, it seemed, was in rushing her fences. She ought to have known a man of Kade's stamp preferred to make the running. If she had played her hand more cautiously, there was no doubt in Josie's mind that she would have been successful in her quest. Kade might be hard, but he was still very much a man.

Her musings were broken off by her grandfather, who appeared by her side, and Josie, hoping he had had enough, waited to hear him say so, and was only too ready to accompany him home. Again she was disappointed as he said complainingly, 'Let's find us somewhere to park. There ought to be some seating somewhere.'

His voice told Josie that he was getting tired, and she tried to capitalise on this by suggesting they made tracks for home. This suggestion did not receive the hoped-for reaction, as he gave her a suspicious look under beetling eyebrows. 'Thought girls liked parties,' he commented.

Josie sighed. He intended to stick it out come what may, and that meant that he had an object in mind, and Josie didn't need two guesses to know what. Well, as long as she stayed with him his hopes of a quiet talk with Kade would receive the same treatment as most of her hopes had where that man was concerned.

When the band struck up shortly after the welcoming speech had been given, Josie sat watching the dancers. Dan had now joined them and sat next to Joseph. Not being able to dance, Josie felt reasonably sure of her ability to stay close to her grandfather, and when the vacant seat next to her was taken by a stout lady, she felt even more secure.

The lady turned out to be Mrs Carver, who, knowing that Josie was a friend of Lucy's, told her that Lucy would be along a little later on, having had to wait until her baby-sitter turned up.

So far, so good, thought Josie as she chatted amiably with Mrs Carver, noting the way Jessica had suddenly left her group of friends and headed across the room towards another small clutch of people, and where Josie presumed Kade was being kept entertained.

No sooner had the thought come that she would be able to fend off any attempt by Kade to seek either her company or her grandfather's than he was standing in front of her requesting, with that wicked grin of his, the dance now starting up.

Josie had no hesitation in answering, 'Oh, dear, I'm sorry, but I don't dance.'

Kade raised his eyebrows at this, and her grandfather, looking from Kade to Josie, growled, 'Danged if I know what she did with her time over there, Boston, apart from studying.'

Josie coloured, absolutely furious with her grandfather, for he had managed to let her know he was disappointed with her, and also managed to get in an oblique reference to her profession, confirming her suspicion that he meant to tackle Kade on what he thought had been an omission on his part in not nominating her for a school post.

Seeing her discomfiture, Kade smoothly assured her grandfather that it was refreshing to meet someone who was dedicated to her profession, leaving Josie with an impression of a double-edged compliment, that could be either sarcasm or simple fact, and she couldn't decide which.

At this point Mrs Carver exclaimed quickly, 'Oh, there's my husband. He's not much of a one for party affairs, so I'd better go and join him before he bolts for the door.'

It was all Josie could do not to grab her hand and force her to sit down again, for her exit left an empty chair beside her and Kade had showed no sign of moving on.

She might have known it, she thought miserably as Kade settled down beside her in a manner that suggested that he had been waiting for just such an opportunity, and very probably had, she mused unhappily.

In no time Jessica was approaching them, and Kade was forced to stand up again as it was obvious she wanted a word with him. 'Now don't settle too long, Kade,' she said in a low husky voice. 'Remember we've arranged to have a meeting about the opening ceremony.' Her glance of mute appeal left Kade and rested on Josie, and her eyes narrowed speculatively. 'What a pity you won't be joining the school,' she said spitefully, adding maliciously, 'I'm sure you'll find something, though, talent is always needed.'

Josie's hands clenched, and she heard Kade reply in a low furious voice, 'Don't worry your head about Miss West, Miss Hanway. Her talent will quite definitely not be wasted, I can assure you.'

It was Jessica's turn to look discomfited, and with set lips she again reminded him about the meeting, to which Kade replied in an almost insolent voice, 'As it's only a preliminary meeting, I'm sure you can manage without me. Just let me have the minutes, and I'll let you have my comments.'

A dull red flush stained Jessica's features, and Josie felt really sorry for her, but she had asked for all she had got. She was pushing again, and as before she had come up against an immovable object, Kade! In this she had Josie's sympathy, who knew just how she felt.

As Jessica swept away, barely attempting to hide the fact that she was furious, Josie saw her grandfather glance at Kade. There was admiration and satisfaction in that glance, and she knew he wouldn't rest until he found out just what Kade had in mind for her—jobwise, that was—for his remarks had left little room for doubt that he did have an object in view.

Josie's hands clenched tighter as an answer to Kade's extraordinary statement hit her. So that was it! He was hoping to make a deal with her grandfather about her future—on a certain understanding, of course! No wonder he had told her to forget Carella! She must have been blind not to have seen what he had in mind.

Now that she had worked that out, it was of vital importance that her grandfather was not given a chance of a private word with Kade. No matter what, Josie wasn't going to move from his side. The next thing she knew, Lucy was walking over to her with an expression on her face not unlike her grandfather's a moment ago. She must have witnessed Jessica's furious exit from the scene and put her own interpretation on it.

When Kade got to his feet at her approach, Josie knew that he would have to offer his chair to Lucy, and felt a surge of relief that quickly turned to dismay as her grandfather, stealing a march on her, idly suggested to Kade that they ought to try a beer, a suggestion that met with instant approval from an amused Kade, who had not missed Josie's dilemma at the turn of events.

He knows, thought Josie furiously, as her apprehensive eyes went from her grandfather now leading the way to the bar section, and the tall, broad figure of Kade following him, with Dan bringing up the rear. He knew that she'd worked it out, but he didn't care one jot for anyone's feelings—or the fact that he was playing on an old man's wish for his niece's happiness.

She was so engrossed in her thoughts she did not hear the first part of Lucy's comments as she settled herself down next to her. 'Josie, don't you dare ever tell me Kade is a hard man!' she exclaimed. 'I could kiss him for what he did just then. I didn't hear quite what that woman said to you, but I did hear Kade's reply—and so did quite a lot of folk. I told you she was a trier, didn't I? and brazen with it. But even she must have got the message by now—as well as half the townsfolk!'

Josie did not reply to this, and let Lucy happily ramble on. Her attention was riveted on the other end of the room, where her grandfather and Kade had drawn apart from the rest of the gathering round the bar and were having a long discussion.

If her grandfather agreed to the proposition Josie was sure Kade was now putting to him, she would never speak to him again, she thought wildly. He was a fine one to talk about pride when he was willing to agree to such a deal!

Lucy stayed with her until the men returned, and giving Josie's hand a slight squeeze she said that she ought to be making tracks back, as her sitter hadn't turned up, and Nat was holding the fort, and that he'd never forgive her if the beer ran out before he got there.

With another of those enigmatical looks of his, Kade settled down next to Josie again, and in a bland voice asked her how things were going at the school, and he trusted Maryanne had apologised for her bad behaviour.

Josie, hard put to it not to scream at him that Maryanne and the rest of the entourage at Blue Mount could jump off the Empire State Building for all she cared, somehow managed an answer. As her grandfather had elected to stay at the bar talk-

ing to a colleague of his, Josie, seeing that Dan's
attention was being held by the mayor who had
come across to have a word with him, took the bull
by the horns, and meeting Kade's amused eyes
demanded, 'What did you say to my grandfather?'

Kade's brows lifted at this bald attack. 'What
should I have said to him?' he countermanded
blandly, then frowned as if concentrating, but
Josie wasn't fooled. 'I think,' he went on deliber-
atingly, 'I thanked him for the fine speech he gave
on my arrival.' His now mocking eyes met Josie's.
'Satisfied?' he queried softly.

Josie flushed and looked away quickly. She
might have known she wouldn't get a straight
answer; she couldn't expect him to show her the
ace he held in the silent and extremely unfair
game they were playing.

When the mayor turned his attention to Kade
and drew him into a discussion on town affairs,
Josie breathed a sigh of relief, and catching her
grandfather's eye from across the room gave a
quick nod in answer to his suggestive look towards
the door, asking her if she were ready to leave.
Josie was more than ready, and murmuring a swift,
'Goodnight,' to anyone who happened to be listening, and Kade was, as he immediately turned towards her and got to his feet, saying in what
sounded like a rueful voice, 'Must you go so early?'

'My grandfather tires easily,' she answered
coldly, adding, 'He's no longer as strong as he
was—or as young,' managing to inject much em-
phasis on the last word for Kade's benefit, then she
turned away quickly before he could say anything
else.

Nat was waiting by the door to take them back to Carella, for as Dan had offered to pick them up, he had arranged for his son to take them home, knowing that Joseph would be leaving long before the end of the party.

As Nat was with them, Josie had to hold back the questions she was longing to put to her grandfather and wait until they arrived home. When they said goodnight to Nat a few minutes later, she was in a fever of impatience to hear what her grandfather had to say.

'Well?' she demanded, fixing him with an 'I want the truth' look. 'Just what did Kade mean when he said my talents wouldn't be wasted? And don't tell me you have no idea what I'm talking about,' she warned him swiftly, knowing that innocent look of his. 'I saw you buttonhole him after you lured him to the bar.'

Joseph West grinned, and rubbed a horny hand over his chin. 'Seems you caught me redhanded, sheriff,' he growled, putting both hands in the air.

Instead of laughing at her grandfather's favourite trick of amusing her when she was young, Josie could have cried, for she knew with absolute certainty that whatever he had learned from Kade Boston he was going to keep himself, and no amount of persuasion would prise it out of him.

Swallowing a lump in her throat, she gave him a half-smile and turned towards the stairs to show him that she understood. 'Goodnight, Gramps,' she said in a low voice with the weariness showing through, as did the way she held her head. She was beaten. Kade had won, as she had known he would.

Her grandfather's voice stopped her as her foot touched the first rung of the stairs. 'No call for the miseries, girl,' he ordered. 'You ought to be right proud that Kade's got work lined up for you. He'll see you right, just as I thought he would.'

Josie turned and looked back at her grandfather. So he had made a deal with him, and it must have been much as she had thought. For her future he had signed away Carella! No wonder Kade had been so pleased with himself. 'Oh, Gramps!' she cried, not being able to bear it a moment longer. 'Can't you see why he's helping me? He's helping himself, too, it's Carella he's really after.'

Her grandfather blinked at her in astonishment, then a slow smile lit up his features. 'I know that, don't I?' he said happily, just as if it were of no consequence, and gave the astounded Josie another shock by adding, 'And I've a notion to hand it to him on a plate after the way he shot that little besom down in flames tonight.'

And that was as much as Josie was going to hear, for before she could attempt to ask him any more questions, he had muttered, 'Sleep well, girl,' and was on his way into the sitting-room to get his usual nightcap.

CHAPTER TEN

JOSIE did not fall asleep until the early hours of
the morning, and then only through sheer ex-
haustion. Her mind was too active to allow her to
fall into the state of tranquillity so necessary for
sleep.

Her grandfather's advice that she had nothing to
worry about proved a fallacy, and had caused her
more worry. How Kade had got her grandfather's
approval, not to mention the happy way he was
considering actually giving him Carella, Josie was
at a loss to understand, and she suspected he had
made some reference to the state of the homestead.
Although this was much improved since Josie's
return, it was still a large house, and Kade would
only have to refer obliquely to the fact that it must
have been hard for her to manage, and keep a job
as well. As these were much the same thoughts that
her grandfather had had, such a reference would
strike an immediate chord with him, and, thought
Josie miserably, pave the way for the success of
Kade's enterprises.

Turning restlessly over on to her side, she wondered what sort of a job Kade had got lined up for
her this time. The children would shortly be going
to the new school, so her work as a teacher would
be finished. Even Maryanne was going, for she had
told Josie that her parents were expected back
about a week before the start of the fall term.

Josie sighed. There had to be an answer somewhere. The work would have to be in the teaching line, for she couldn't see her grandfather agreeing to a deal otherwise. Her mind went back to Blue Mount. It had to be something connected with the ranch, for there was no other school she could work at.

The answer came quite suddenly, and Josie wondered why she hadn't thought of it before. She would still teach—not children this time, but their fathers! Hadn't Kade said something about them not being able to read or write, and how the children had shown signs of following in their footsteps? He had also said that although they felt that way now, they would regret it later. So—mused Josie, something the men had said must have given Kade this insight into their feelings.

If this work was in fact what he had in mind, she found she had no objection. It wasn't quite what she had been trained for, but it was needed nevertheless. She frowned. Was it really worth Carella? And for how long would it last? Not all that long, she told herself, for she doubted if there were more than half a dozen hands in need of such help—and what then? Had Kade plans of starting up a kindergarten for the rest of his employees' children? Was she to spend her time wondering what other work he would find her when each avenue dried up—work that he would deem suitable for her talent—the talent he had so strongly assured Jessica Hanway would not be wasted?

No, no, no! she repeated vehemently to herself. She would not be a puppet—Kade's or anyone else's! Her grandfather might think he was doing the right thing for her, but he didn't know what had gone before—or how Josie had got herself tangled with Kade in the first place.

He could have Carella! It didn't belong to her anway, and if her grandfather decided to sell, then there was nothing she could do about it, but she would not be a party to the deal. It was unfair of her grandfather making her one, and all because of a wretched job!

On this thought she sat straight up in bed. It was because he wanted her settled that he had been willing to listen to Kade's proposition—and Kade had known this, and played on it. What if Josie found her own job? Dallas wasn't all that far away, and she did have a car now. Her eyes gleamed. So it might not be teaching—not at first anyway, but if she could find something that would rank as a suitable occupation in the eyes of her grandfather ... Her thoughts ran on; why not try for a position as a governess? Surely they had them there as they did everywhere else. Some parents preferred their children to receive private tuition. Her heart lifted as she considered the probabilities in front of her. Oh, why hadn't she thought of this before and not allowed herself to become enmeshed at Blue Mount? But it wasn't too late now; all she had to do was go to Dallas and make a few enquiries as to the likelihood of her gaining such employment. There were bound to be agencies that catered for her profession. The eager look in her eyes vanished for a moment as she considered the fact that she would have to spend the week away from her grandfather, returning at the weekends, and she couldn't see this state of affairs pleasing him, but she had no choice—not now. At least there would be a faint hope that he would decide against selling Carella, for there would no longer be a reason for him to do so.

There was just five weeks left for Josie to find herself employment, and each weekend would be used for this purpose. From now on her Saturdays would be spent in Dallas, going round the agencies. If she was lucky she might get suited at her first call. She sighed; it would be so wonderful if she were. To be able to tell her grandfather that she had got a job, and would not be requiring the help of Kade Boston or anyone else, would give her a great deal of pleasure, not to mention her satisfaction when telling Kade.

She was now grateful that she did not know the ins and outs of the proposition her grandfather had made with Kade, and in this case, ignorance was bliss, for she could go ahead with a clear conscience and make her own arrangements. She would have to make some excuse for the Dallas visit, though, for she had no intention of telling her grandfather what she intended to do—it might force him to reveal the pact he had made with Kade, and Josie would then be under an obligation to help him keep it.

It was something her grandfather said at breakfast that gave her a perfect excuse for her visit to Dallas, for he had been talking about the party the evening before, and how Josie ought to attend more social occasions. 'All work and no play isn't much of a life, girl, and from what I can gather you've done your share of work, over there as well as here.' Josie knew he was referring to the fact that she could not dance, and knew that it had worried him. 'Dan's got a woman that goes in and cleans up for him twice a week.' He cleared his throat. 'Been thinking of getting someone for us— take the polishing work off your hands, anyway.' He looked up at Josie, who was watching him with a wary look in her eyes, and coughed again. 'Anyway, we'll keep it in mind.'

At her, 'Very well, Gramps,' he shot her a suspicious look, and Josie went on quickly to say, 'I'll have to get a few more dresses in, I suppose, for these social occasions you seem to think I ought to attend. I was thinking of doing some shopping in Dallas,' she added idly, and shot her grandfather a surreptitious look to see how he took this.

His reply quite startled her. 'Now that's more like it!' he said briskly. 'And don't you worry about getting back early to fix me a meal. I managed okay on my own before, and it won't hurt me to get myself something.'

It was Josie's turn to look suspicious. Kade must have laid it on thick, she thought furiously, to produce this sort of response from her grandfather.

He was so pleased that she was spending the day on what he called a 'shopping spree' that Josie felt downright mean about the scheme she had in mind, and as she sat in the State bus that she was able to pick up outside the township, she found herself hoping her quest was unsuccessful, for this trip anyway!

Dallas was forty miles from the township, and while she gazed out at the passing landscape, Josie reflected that it wasn't all that far to travel, and she might, she thought, even be able to stay at

Carella if she could get a job in Dallas itself—always providing, she told herself darkly, that her grandfather didn't conclude the deal with Kade.

As the bus neared its destination and they entered the intersections leading off the main highway, Josie stared in consternation at the swiftly moving lanes ahead of them. She would never negotiate her way through that! It was bus or nothing, she thought bleakly, and even a large sign that categorically stated, 'DALLAS IS BEAUTIFUL' failed to raise her crestfallen spirits, for she had a sudden vision of Blue Mount, and the practically deserted byroads that led to the ranch, and the wonderful feeling of space that she would get as she drove there each morning.

For one fleeting moment she was tempted to forget her well-intentioned scheme and leave her fate in the hands of Kade, to do as he wished with her, and her eyes pricked at the thought. If she hadn't fallen in love with him then perhaps it might have been possible—but not now, not after the way he had gone about obtaining Carella, using her to gain his objective. Her pride alone wouldn't allow her to accept this, and she would far rather be out of his vicinity altogether, even though, she mused, it meant joining that thick stream of traffic that rushed along as if the occupants of the cars hadn't a moment to live—even that was preferable.

Before leaving the bus terminal Josie checked on the return trips and found they were not as frequent as she had thought they would be, for there were two-hourly intervals between each bus, and she decided to catch the eight o'clock one back. Not that she wanted to wait that long before her return, but she had to humour her grandfather, although she couldn't think how he expected her to fill her time after the stores had closed. Perhaps he had thought she might take in a movie, she shrugged lightly; his main concern had been that if she was in Dallas, or anywhere else come to that, she wouldn't be doing the endless chores she filled her weekends with, catching up on the week's housework.

After negotiating her way to the main shopping areas, where she hoped to find the agencies she was seeking, Josie ruminated that her grandfather hadn't been all that far off the mark when he had suggested she made a day of it, for it was almost lunch time before she had found what looked as if it might be a promising start to her job quest, and although the agency advertised office vacancies, she felt it was worth a try.

However, a few minutes later she found that office vacancies were all they had, but she did have some success, for the helpful manager gave her an address of an agency to try on the other side of the city.

Worried that the firm might close for the lunch period, Josie caught a cab to take her to her destination, and was devoutly glad that she did, for on arrival at the given address she found that the firm had moved their premises—back to where she had just come from!—and just managed to stop the cab taking off again, and got the cheery cab driver to make the return journey.

Paying the cabby off, she started the foot-weary tramp down a narrow side street, to the number given on the board outside the old premises, with a nasty feeling that fate was ganging up on her and try as she might she would be unsuccessful in her quest. At this thought she squared her slim shoulders. Getting despondent wouldn't help, and at least this agency handled the type of post she was seeking.

Five minutes later, however, her lightened spirits received a severe setback as she gazed at a 'closed' sign hung up in the window of the agency.

'Wouldn't you know it!' exclaimed an exasperated voice behind her, and Josie turned to meet the rueful eyes of a youngish-looking girl with a pony-style hairdo that swung from side to side as she spoke. 'I guess it never occurs to them that some of us have to work during the week, and this is the only time we can get to visit,' she said in a soft Southern drawl. 'You on the same rounds?' she queried.

Josie nodded slowly. 'I was told they handled my work' she said wearily, her voice showing her disappointment.

The girl started at Josie's accent. 'You're English?' she enquired.

Josie smiled at her. 'American,' she answered, 'brought up in England, I've only been home a few months.'

The girl held out her hand. 'Patsy Hather,' she said. 'I guess I can take it we're both teachers?'

Josie took her hand and gave her name, adding, 'Pleased to meet you, Patsy, and I suppose I can take it that you're looking for a job too?' she tacked on dryly.

Patsy nodded, making the ponytail bounce even higher, and sighed as she looked back at the Closed

sign. 'I've been looking for two months now—
writing off to various colleges, but had no luck so
far.' She looked back at Josie and wrinkled her
nose. 'No experience, you see,' she sighed again.
'I'm ready for them, but they're not ready for me,
I guess,' she complained.

As if mutually agreed, the girls started walking
back to the main town area, and when they passed
a drugstore, Patsy suggested they had a milk shake,
unless Josie had another appointment, of course.

Josie hadn't, and was quite willing to dally away
the time with her new-found friend, for it turned
out that Patsy's situation was much the same as
hers, in that she too had come from a small town,
and like Josie had had to seek work in a city, although in her case there was no nearby school.
The children were on 'bussing' schedules, and
some, Patsy told her, went as far as thirty miles,
according to their grade.

It was natural that the two girls should team up
for the rest of the day. Patsy, like Josie, hadn't
fancied a day on her own in the city, yet hadn't
wanted to go home early.

To salve her conscience, Josie did buy a dress,
one that could be worn for special occasions, but
not too fancy, although she had no idea what occasion the dress would eventually be used for.

It was through Patsy that Josie missed her bus,
not only the one she had meant to catch, but the
following one too. In their tour of the city, they
had come across a movie house that was showing a
film that had received wide acclamation, and both
girls had felt that it was a chance not to be missed,

now that they were in what they referred to as 'civilisation'.

Emerging from a dimly-lit foyer a few hours later, and blinking hard to accustom their eyes to the glare of the afternoon sun, the girls walked down the steps leading to the exit and Patsy missed the last step. Before Josie could prevent her falling, she had sprawled on to the sidewalk.

Seeing her wince as she helped her up, Josie inquired anxiously if she had hurt herself, and Patsy, trying to make light of the accident, gave a wry grimace as she shifted the weight of her left leg and examined the badly grazed knee and hopelessly torn tights.

'I think we'd better have that seen to,' commented Josie, keeping a supporting arm around Patsy's waist, and hailing a cruising taxi, she got the driver to take them to the nearest casualty centre.

Within a remarkably short time, Patsy's knee had been attended to, and she was given a tetanus injection for good measure. Her right arm, too, had come under medical scrutiny as she had sprained her wrist as she had attempted to break her fall.

By the time the girls had left the casualty centre, Josie found herself accompanying not only a limping Patsy, but a one-armed Patsy, for her right arm had been enclosed in a sling.

When Patsy asked Josie what time her bus was due to leave, Josie countermanded the question by wanting to know when Patsy's bus left. This query forced a grin from Patsy, who was in no doubt of Josie's intentions. 'Honestly, Josie, I'll be okay. I'm sure your bus leaves before mine. Mine are few and far between, and I'll not get one now until after ten.'

'How long after ten?' persisted Josie, determined not to leave Patsy until she had seen her safely on the bus.

'Thirty after,' answered Patsy, 'and I don't know where that leaves you. For all we know, your connections might fold after ten, and there's no need for you to stay with me.'

'I'm staying,' replied Josie firmly, not failing to notice the other girl's pallor and guessing she must have been in a certain amount of pain, not to mention discomfort, with her arm in a ·sling. 'There's such a thing as trains, I presume?' she queried with a lift of her finely arched eyebrows.

Patsy's good arm came round Josie's slim waist. 'You're a brick, Josie, but I've my doubts. I think you'll find they're trucking rails, and you'd get stuck in the middle of nowhere. Tell you what,' she suggested brightly, 'we'll make enquiries at the depot, and if you've a bus that leaves shortly after mine, then I'd be surely grateful for your company—if not, then it's no go.'

Josie knew full well that her next bus after Patsy's connection would leave at midnight, but did not say so. Somehow she had to prevent this fact from coming to Patsy's notice, and when they arrived at the depot and saw the long line of people waiting to be attended to at the information kiosk, Josie breathed a sigh of relief. Patsy was in no state to stand in that line, and seeing her comfortably seated in one of the chairs that were provided for waiting passengers, Josie took her place in the line.

'It's all right,' she assured Patsy later when she rejoined her, 'there's a bus that leaves fifteen minutes after yours. How's that?' she said triumphantly.

'Are you sure?' demanded Patsy suspiciously. 'You're not kidding me, are you?'

Opening her blue eyes in feigned indignation, Josie replied, 'Of course not!' asking for the lie to be forgiven.

That settled, the girls made their way to the refreshment bay, and over a light meal Patsy told Josie about her home background.

'It's not been easy for Mother, you know,' she confided. 'Dad walked out on us when we were young, and she had to fend for us. It couldn't have been easy for her letting me stay on for graduation, but she wouldn't hear of me giving up and helping out with the income by getting a job of some sort. I'm the eldest, you see.' She sighed. 'I guess it's going to come to that yet, in spite of Mom's hopes for me. She works in a store and comes home dead beat, and it kinda hurts seeing her like that, and me not able to help out. It wouldn't matter so much if I could get some kind of vacation job, and if there's one listed, I always seem to get there either just after the job's been taken, or there are ten or more in front of me, and I never even get to the interview,' she added despondently, then looked at Josie. 'How about you?' she asked.

Josie told her about her background, passing lightly over the years she had spent in England, and explained how she had been fortunate in finding a job soon after coming home, and when she mentioned the job she had been given at Blue Mount, Patsy gave a sigh of pure envy. 'Gosh, Josie, you sure fell on your feet!' Then it suddenly occurred to her that Josie was seeking a job. 'Did it fold up?' she asked.

Josie shook her head, 'No, it didn't fold up. I suppose I just wanted a change,' she lied, and seeing the look of incredulity this produced on Patsy, went on to say, 'Well, things were a bit complicated,' leaving Patsy to draw her own conclusions, and this she apparently did by giving Josie a long appraisal and summing up her conclusions by a dry, 'I guess with your looks you'll always have some sort of problem, the men go for dewy-eyed blondes,' she tacked on with a grin.

'It was nothing like that,' protested Josie indignantly, and shrugged. 'I just wasn't happy,' she ended lamely, thinking that it was the truth, not the whole truth, but near enough to satisfy Patsy.

Patsy sighed again. 'Well, I hope you haven't made a mistake by throwing the job up, that's all. They don't grow on trees, Josie.'

This time Josie echoed her sigh. 'I'm beginning to find that out,' she agreed dolefully.

The girls stayed at the bus depot, for there was now only an hour to go before Patsy's bus departed, and Patsy was only too happy to stay put. At least there was somewhere to sit down, and it was obvious that if they moved they would soon lose their seats, for the waiting rooms were gradually filling up with fellow passengers.

At Patsy's instigation, Josie rang her grandfather and explained that she would be late home, telling him not to worry, and that she had had a lovely day. She had thought of doing this earlier, but had been afraid that Patsy would be suspicious again, and hadn't wanted to risk it, but as Patsy had rung her mother and put her into the picture, Josie had no choice but to follow her example.

There were just ten minutes to go before Patsy's bus departed when Josie, idly watching the continual stream of outgoing and incoming human traffic, stiffened in her seat as her eyes met Kade's grey ones as he stood surveying her from the other side of the crowded room, and she watched in a kind of stupefied fascination as he covered the distance between them in a matter of seconds, and was collecting her one and only package and all but lifting her out of her seat before she had fully recovered her aplomb.

Resisting his hold on her arm, Josie turned to Patsy and took full note of the 'Wow!' expression in her eyes as she studied Kade. 'Patsy, this is Mr Boston,' she introduced hastily. 'Er ... a friend of my grandfather's,' she added lamely, not wanting to say 'my employer', and did not miss the sardonic look this brought from Kade, and felt the familiar surge of temper towards him. What right had he got to just sweep in and pick her up as if she were his property? 'Patsy's bus doesn't go until ten-thirty,' she said coldly, 'and although I presume you're offering me a lift back home, I'm afraid I'm not leaving until I've seen her off.'

Kade gave his lazy grin at this, making Patsy's eyes open yet wider. 'Hi, Patsy,' he drawled, then nodded towards her arm. 'Had an argument with someone?' he queried, his eyes taking in the thick strip of plaster over her knee and the torn stocking.

Patsy grinned and tossed her ponytail back in an arch movement, and Josie felt exasperated. He apparently had that effect on all the girls. 'Not quite,' supplied Patsy. 'I guess I'm accident-prone,' she added sadly, then looked from Kade to Josie. 'Go ahead, Josie, I'll be okay—honest.'

Josie shook her head firmly and stared at Kade. 'I'm staying. The bus might be late, and as you can see she's in no state to be left on her own.'

Kade's thoughtful glance went from Josie back to Patsy again. 'Where are you heading, Patsy?' he asked.

Patsy gave the name of the small town, and her eyes opened to their full extent when Kade casually remarked, 'I know of it. We'll do a round trip and drop you off,' and without waiting for either girl's comments on this bald statement, he had rounded them up and was ushering them out of the bus terminal.

To Patsy's awed whisper of, 'Does he always act like this?' to Josie as they found themselves shepherded towards a gleaming Jaguar drawn up outside the depot, Josie gave a short, 'Always!' the exasperation she felt plainly showing by the vehement answer, Patsy gave her a curious glance.

It was like being in the wake of a hurricane, Josie mused furiously, as the car glided smoothly out on to the highway. She didn't understand how Kade came to be in Dallas or how he knew that she was there, or where to find her. Her smouldering eyes rested on his thick hair, noticing almost absently how it curled slightly at the ends, not too long, yet not too short. As she had elected to sit in the back with Patsy, she was able to get a close picture of the back of his head, studying him without his knowledge. It was a fine head, almost leonine, she thought, but then he was a proud man, and very much a king of his own domain.

Her eyes left his head and she looked out of the window in front of her, then as if compelled, towards the driving mirror just above Kade's head, and she knew a sense of utter frustration when her eyes met his. So he had known she had been studying him!

'I was with your grandfather when you called through,' he said casually, telling Josie that he had correctly assessed her earlier thoughts. Nothing more was said on this point, but it gave Josie much food for thought.

As they neared Patsy's home town, Patsy gave directions to Kade after he had refused to drop her at the nearest point and insisted on going the whole way. At this Josie was relieved, for Patsy had been a little vague as to precisely where she lived in the town, and Josie had suspected that it was a little further than she would have wanted the other girl to walk in her condition. That Kade was of the same opinion was proved by his insistence on taking her all the way.

When they eventually reached the town and Patsy told Kade to turn off the main street and down a side street and eventually out the other side of the town, Josie was given confirmation of her earlier suspicions. The houses they passed were grouped together in small clumps, and Josie could see they were in what might be termed as 'out of town' areas.

All this time Patsy talked profusely about this and that, and how she would like to hear from Josie on how she fared on the job-hunting quest, and perhaps they might even land up at the same school, making Josie seriously consider taking the plaster off her knee and placing it on her mouth, but she managed to answer politely enough.

On reaching Patsy's home, Kade saw her to the door, and within minutes Josie was being ushered into the house by a very relieved Mrs Hather, and sitting down in the shabby but clean living room accepting a cup of coffee.

To Josie's discomfort, Patsy related how they had met, and had to listen to Mrs Hather's sympathetic remarks on how Patsy was having the same trouble in getting fixed up with work, and Kade sitting there looking so relaxed, taking it all in and not saying a word. Josie didn't know which was the more embarrassing, but after a second's thought she did know, and shrank further into her chair when she remembered what she had said about the job she did have!

This time, however, fate smiled kindly on her, for Kade abruptly terminated any further discussion by declaring that they must be on their way, and Josie all but ran to the door.

Although she would have preferred to have sat in the back seat, Kade gave her no opportunity by opening the front passenger door and waiting for her to get in. The car door closed on her with an ominous tight click, and Josie knew a feeling of panic, for which she roundly scolded herself. He had to know some time that she wasn't going to be coerced into accepting whatever work he had got lined up for her—but she wished he hadn't found out this way. It wasn't as if she had been successful, she thought miserably, and could tell him without fear or favour that she had another post to go to. Hearing Patsy's tale of woe hadn't helped either, she mused bitterly, but it would certainly give Kade an added incentive to push home his offer of employment.

The miles slipped by and Josie waited apprehensively for the inevitable questions, and sneaking a quick glance at the silent Kade beside her, found herself puzzled by his apparent absorption of the road ahead, yet she knew his thoughts were elsewhere, and somehow sensed they were not on her.

His almost conversational, 'I think we'll be able to offer Patsy a job, we're still short-staffed at the school,' was his first remark. He was silent for a second or so, then went on in the same casual tone, 'Have to find her lodgings, of course, but I guess she won't mind that.'

A shocked Josie found herself wondering if he expected her to endorse this suggestion, and looked away out of the window. She was glad for Patsy, of course, she told herself fiercely, and she did need a job, more so than Josie did, but that wasn't the point. Kade hadn't given her a chance to apply for a post—hadn't even bothered to recommend her—and, she reminded herself tightly, he had actually told Miss Plumstead that she wasn't interested! She swallowed hard. Yet here he was offering a post to a total stranger—why, she thought wildly, Patsy might have robbed her grandfather and grandmother for all he knew, yet he didn't care—it was just her, Josie, that he'd got it in for.

'Well, don't you think it's a good idea?' he enquired smoothly, rubbing the salt in the wound. Josie acknowledged silently.

'A very good idea, she managed to answer, making her voice as casual as his. 'She's a very sweet girl, and she hasn't had an easy time of it by the look of things.' It was true, she told herself relentlessly, she oughtn't to begrudge Patsy a chance—her good luck was Josie West's bad luck.

'Now about this job you're trying to get,' he began airily, and Josie clenched her teeth. If he as much as dared to advise her to stay on at Blue Mount ... 'I wouldn't bother,' he went on inexorably. 'I've already told you, I've plans for you.' He gave her a swift look, then paid attention to the road again. 'The trouble with you is, you don't listen to what you're told,' he added musingly, then shot out at her, 'Why do you think I stopped you from getting a job at the new school?'

Josie's hands clenched into small fists. 'I don't have to ask why,' she replied bitterly. 'I know why, so I can see no point in wasting my breath by asking.'

'You'll be lucky if you have any breath left by the time I've finished with you,' he growled ominously, and still more ominously pulled up in a layby and sat looking at her.

After giving him one defiant look Josie looked away from him and out to the twinkling lights of a nearby town. 'It's all right,' she said wearily, suddenly tired of the whole wretched business. 'You don't have to explain anything.' She looked back at him, still keeping that close watch on her. 'You don't usually dot the i's, do you? So why bother now? Tell me one thing,' she said scathingly, 'would I have got the job at the school if I'd helped you get Carella?'

The swift indrawn breath told her she was treading on dangerous ground, but she didn't care. 'No!' he bit out harshly. 'There was just no way that you'd have got any job, let alone the school job.'

It was Josie's turn to draw in a quick breath; well, she had asked for it, hadn't she? 'Thank you,' she said quietly. 'Do you mind if we go now? I'm sure my grandfather will be wondering where I've got to.'

'Don't you want to know why I won't let you get a job?' he asked softly.

Here we go again, thought Josie tiredly, and he was accusing her of not listening to what he said! Her silence gave him the go-ahead. He seemed determined to tell her, and sick as she was with the whole subject, she might as well let him get it over with.

'I want to marry you,' he said, giving her a hard look as if daring her to interrupt him, 'and while I hold moderate views on quite a number of subjects, no wife of mine works for anyone else. Not,' he added grandly, 'that she'll have time. I intend to make quite sure of that.'

Josie's first stunned thoughts, when she was able to think, that was, was that Kade must have wanted Carella more than she had realised, then common sense took over. He wasn't the sort of man to go that far. 'How long have you had this in mind?' she asked in a voice decidedly unlike her own.

Kade grinned wickedly. 'Ever since you told me I ought to be ashamed of myself for bullying an old man,' he drawled. 'Took me back to my schooldays—you just had to be a schoolmarm. The rest was easy.'

Josie stared at him. 'The rest?' she asked, trying to sound casual, but her feelings gave her away and it came out in a kind of squeak.

Again Kade grinned. 'Maryanne,' he said gently. 'She was due back the week I met you. I cabled her parents for permission to keep her with me. She'd been booked in at a Houston boarding school, and she hadn't been looking forward to it, so there was no problem in telling her that she was to stay with me.'

Josie looked down at her hands; it didn't seem possible, yet he had no reason to lie to her. 'You didn't give me the impression of being struck with me when I spoke to you in the main street,' she said in a small uncertain voice.

'Ah, yes,' drawled Kade. 'But I hadn't quite got you figured then, but I guessed if I riled you enough you'd offer to pay for that fencing—and you did.'

Josie drew in a deep breath. 'You knew I'd put that fence up, didn't you?' she challenged him.

He nodded. 'Your grandfather might be getting on in years, but he's not that old,' he drawled softly.

Josie swallowed. 'You mean to tell me that I worried myself sick over the possibility of you having a row with Gramps over it, and you sit there and calmly tell me ...' She was lost for words for a second or so, then asked curiously, 'What would you have done if I hadn't offered to pay for the fencing?'

'Sent you a whacking big bill,' he replied casually. 'To the store, of course,' he added wickedly. 'You don't think I called in the store that day by accident, do you?'

Josie's wide eyes studied him. She hadn't thought of that, Lucy had told her that he rarely came to town. 'Taking a chance, weren't you? Tangling with a gold-digger?' she asked in a small bitter voice. 'You must have heard what the townsfolk were saying about me.'

Kade's mouth hardened. 'I heard,' he said harshly, 'but you never gave me credit for disbelieving the gossip. You still find it hard to see me as an ordinary man, don't you? I've got to be after something, haven't I? If it wasn't Carella, it would be something else, wouldn't it?' he said bitterly. 'Well, just for the record, I've got Carella. Old Joseph saw how it was. We've been working on plans for combining the two properties. If I'd only wanted Carella you could have had that damned school job. Still can,' he added savagely. 'It seems to be all you do want!'

Josie closed her eyes; why had she to spoil everything now? Was it because she couldn't believe that a man as fine as Kade could care for her. 'Kade, I'm sorry—I . . .' she began.

'Forget it,' he said curtly. 'Spare me the "sorry" bit. I'm sorry too—but at least I know where I stand.'

The car engine was switched into life and Josie dumbly watched Kade's strong hands grip the steering wheel and swing the big car back on to the road again. She'd had her chance and completely muffed it. She doubted if she'd ever see him again.

The rest of the journey seemed to last a lifetime. Josie sat huddled in her seat. She wanted to cry, but refused to let herself go. The silence that had fallen between them seemed as impregnable as a wall of steel, and she was powerless to break it.

When eventually the car swung into Carella's drive, Josie had reached rock bottom, and when Kade's hand reached out to unlock her door she stared dully at his lean strong fingers as he jerked the catch back, and before he had had time to draw back, her hand timidly touched his. She wanted to tell him she loved him, but the words wouldn't come, and this was the only way she felt she could convey her feelings to him, but her breath caught in her throat when he gently removed her hand from his, as if to say, 'Don't feel bad about it. I understand.'

Her throat was dry when she got out of the car, and she summoned all her will power to say, 'Thank you, Kade, for everything,' and rushed for the door. If he had really loved her he would have understood her small but telling action, but he hadn't. His pride had got in the way.

Her hand was on the door catch when she was swung round hard and into his arms before she could draw breath, and being kissed in no uncertain manner. 'Damn you ...' he said against her bruised lips. 'Tell me you love me! You didn't think I'd let you go, did you?' He shook her, his fingers bruising her shoulders. 'Say it out loud,' he commanded.

Josie had barely enough breath to comply, and it

came out in a whisper, but Kade wasn't satisfied, 'Louder,' he ordered in his autocratic way. 'I want the whole town to hear it.'

She tried again, and it sounded no louder than the last words, but it satisfied Kade, who pulled her close to him again. 'I meant to let you reconsider your position,' he drawled in a teasing tone. 'I thought perhaps a day or so might do the trick.' His voice altered as he said, 'I was pretty sure you felt the same way about me, in spite of the set-downs you kept handing out. You don't think I go around kissing girls, do you? If you're half as bright as your grandfather states you are, you ought to have known I was telling you you belonged to me.'

Josie nestled closer to him and sighed contentedly. She *had* known, or part of her had known. His kiss had been his seal on her, just as she had felt it was, but she had been his long before that, and he had known it. She reached up and kissed his strong jaw. 'And to think,' she whispered, 'I tried so hard not to love you!'

He looked down at her upturned face and kissed her swiftly. 'And don't I know it,' he growled, 'but you hadn't a chance, and I think you knew it.' A thought suddenly struck him then, and he gave her a suspicious look. 'By the way, do you suffer from hay fever?' he asked.

Josie giggled, and received a shake. 'I'm afraid not,' she said with a mischievous look in her eyes. 'I thought you were apologising for not recommending me for a school job.'

Kade grinned. 'In a way, I suppose I was. Er ... it was heart's desire, by the way,' he told her with a twinkle in his eye, 'but as I said, for a teacher it took you a long time to get the message.'

'Well,' murmured Josie consideringly, 'we weren't exactly hitting it off at the time, if I remember rightly. Even so,' she said, as she wound her arms round his waist, 'I did keep them in my bedroom.'

Kade's lips came down on hers as he whispered, 'I'll have a huge bowl of them waiting for you in our room at Blue Mount.'

SAGITTARIUS

Harlequin Horoscope

YOUR LOVE-NATURE
FIRE SIGN   November 22-December 21

Friendly, cheerful, idealistic and enthusiastic, you are always promoting the virtues of something, whether it be a new lover, a new sport you have just taken up, a new diet, or whatever. The trouble is that romance doesn't rate much higher among your enthusiasms than your other interests. Love is not a serious, intense emotion for you; rather, it is a delightful experience you enjoy as long as it doesn't interfere too much with your individuality and freedom. If your lover is demanding, tries to force you into a deeper emotional commitment, you are likely to fade quietly away.

Sagittarius is called the "bachelor sign" because of the lack of strong emotional or sexual needs. On the one hand you see little reason to give up your fun and freedom for marriage. On the other hand you may be swept away by your own impulsive enthusiasm and marry young. If this happens, your adaptability, pride and sense of honor help you make the best of things and the marriage just might succeed. Actually you can be quite happy in a lasting relationship provided your partner shares some of your youthful spirit and wide-ranging interests.

The fire signs—Aries, Leo and your own—share your idealism, optimism, sociability and cheerfulness; the two of you could make a lighthearted, happy pair. The air signs—Libra, Aquarius and Gemini—are also compatible partners because they won't try to hem you in or overwhelm you emotionally.